He finished his call abruptly, then tossed his mobile onto the table next to him. It thunked against the hard wood, making me too aware of the silence.

And too conscious of my own breathing and my mad, clattering heart.

Javier Dos Santos stood there a moment, his attention on the papers before him, or possibly his tablet computer.

When he raised his head, he did it swiftly. His dark eyes were fierce and sure, pinning me where I stood. I understood in a sudden red haze of exposure and fear that he had known I was here all along.

He had known.

"Hello, Imogen," he said, switching to faintly accented English that made my name sound like some kind of incantation. Or terrible curse. "Do you plan to do something more than stare?"

Conveniently Wed!

Conveniently wedded, passionately bedded!

Whether there's a debt to be paid, a will to be obeyed or a business to be saved...she's got no choice but to say, "I do!"

But these billionaire bridegrooms have got another think coming if they imagine marriage will be that easy...

Soon their convenient brides become the objects of inconvenient desire!

Find out what happens after the vows in:

Bound to Her Desert Captor by Michelle Conder

The Greek's Bought Bride by Sharon Kendrick

Claiming His Wedding Night Consequence by Abby Green

Bound by a One-Night Vow by Melanie Milburne

Sicilian's Bride for a Price by Tara Pammi

Claiming His Christmas Wife by Dani Collins

Look for more Conveniently Wed! coming soon!

Caitlin Crews

MY BOUGHT VIRGIN WIFE

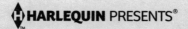

Recycling programs
for this product may
not exist in your area.

ISBN-13: 978-1-335-47797-2

My Bought Virgin Wife

First North American publication 2018

Copyright © 2018 by Caitlin Crews

Printed in U.S.A.

USA TODAY bestselling and RITA® Award–nominated author **Caitlin Crews** loves writing romance. She teaches her favorite romance novels in creative-writing classes at places like UCLA Extension's prestigious Writers' Program, where she finally gets to utilize the MA and PhD in English literature she received from the University of York in England. She currently lives in the Pacific Northwest with her very own hero and too many pets. Visit her at caitlincrews.com.

Books by Caitlin Crews

Harlequin Presents

Undone by the Billionaire Duke

Conveniently Wed!

Imprisoned by the Greek's Ring

One Night With Consequences

A Baby to Bind His Bride
The Guardian's Virgin Ward

Bound to the Desert King

Sheikh's Secret Love-Child

Scandalous Royal Brides

The Prince's Nine-Month Scandal
The Billionaire's Secret Princess

Stolen Brides

The Bride's Baby of Shame

CHAPTER ONE

Imogen

IN THE MORNING I was to marry a monster.

It did not matter what I wanted. It certainly did not matter what I felt. I was the youngest daughter of Dermot Fitzalan, bound in duty to my father's wishes as women in my family had been forever.

I had always known my fate.

But it turned out I was less resigned to it than I'd anticipated when I was younger and far more silly. And when my wedding had not loomed before me, beckoning like some kind of inevitable virus that nothing could keep at bay.

There were no home remedies for my father's wishes.

"You cannot let Father see you in this state, Imogen," my half sister, Celeste, told me briskly as she swept in. "It will only make things worse for you."

I knew she was right. The unfortunate truth was that Celeste was usually right about everything. Elegant, graceful Celeste, who had submitted to her duty with a smile on her face and every appearance of quiet joy. Stunning, universally adored Celeste, who had the willowy blond looks of her late mother and to whom I had forever been compared—and found lacking. My own lost mother had been a titian-haired bombshell, pale of skin and mysteriously emerald of eye, but I resembled her only in the way a fractured reflection, beheld through a mist, might. Next to my half sister, I had always felt like the Fitzalan troll, better suited to a life beneath a bridge somewhere than the grand society life I'd been bred and trained for.

The life Celeste took to with such ease.

Even today, the day before my wedding when theoretically I would be the one looked at, Celeste looked poised and chic in her simple yet elegantly cut clothes. Her pale blond hair was twisted back into an effortless chignon and she'd applied only the faintest hint of cosmetics to enhance her eyes and dramatic cheekbones. While I had yet to change out of my pajamas though it was midday already and I knew without having to look that my curls were in their usual state of disarray.

All of these things seemed filled with more portent than usual, because the monster I was set to marry in the morning had wanted her first.

And likely still wanted her, everyone had whispered.

They had even whispered it to me, and it had surprised me how much it had stung. Because I knew better. My marriage wasn't romantic. I wasn't being chosen by anyone—I was the remaining Fitzalan heiress. My inheritance made me an attractive prospect no matter how irrepressible my hair might have been or how often I disappointed my father with my inability to enhance a room with my decorative presence. I was more likely to draw attention for the wrong reasons.

My laugh was too loud and always inappropriate. My clothes were always slightly askew. I preferred books to carefully vetted social occasions where I was expected to play at hostessing duties. And I had never convinced anyone that I was more fascinated by their interests than my own.

It was lucky, then, that my marriage was about convenience—my father's, not mine. I had never expected anything like a fairy tale.

"Fairy tales are for other families," my severe grandmother had always told us, slamming her marble-edged cane against the hard floors of this sprawling house in the French countryside, where, the story went, our family had been in residence in one form or another since sometime in the twelfth century. "Fitzalans have a higher purpose."

As a child, I'd imagined Celeste and me dressed in armor, riding out to gauzy battles beneath old standards, then slaying a dragon or two before our supper. That had seemed like the kind of higher purpose I could get behind. It had taken the austere Austrian nuns years to teach me that dragon slaying was not the primary occupation of girls from excruciatingly well-blooded old families who were sent away to be educated in remote convents. Special girls with impeccable pedigrees and ambitious fathers had a far different role to fill.

Girls like me, who had never been asked what they might like to do with their lives, because it had all been plotted out already without their input.

The word *pawn* was never used. I had always seen this as a shocking oversight—another opinion of mine that no one had ever solicited and no one wanted to hear.

"You must find purpose and peace in duty, Imogen," Mother Superior had told me, time and again, when I would find myself red-eyed and furious, gritting out another decade of the rosary to atone for my sins. Pride and unnatural self-regard chief among them. "You must cast aside these doubts and trust that those with your best interests at heart have made certain all is as it should be."

"Fitzalans have a higher purpose," Grand-Mère had always said.

By which, I had learned in time, she meant money. Fitzalans hoarded money and made more. This was what had set our family apart across the centuries. Fitzalans were never kings or courtiers. Fitzalans funded kingdoms they liked and overthrew regimes they disparaged, all in service to the expansion of their wealth. This was the grand and glorious purpose that surged in our blood.

"I am not 'in a state,'" I argued to Celeste now, but I didn't sit up or attempt to set myself to rights.

And Celeste did not dignify that with a response.

I had barred myself in the sitting room off my childhood bedchamber, the better to brood at the rain and entertain myself with my enduring fantasies of perfect, beautiful Frederick, who worked in my father's stables and had dreamy eyes of sweetest blue.

We had spoken once, some years ago. He had taken my horse's head and led us into the yard as if I'd required the assistance.

I had lived on the smile he'd given me that day for years.

It seemed unbearable to me that I should find myself staring down so many more years when I would have to do the same, but worse, in the company of a man—a *husband*—who was hated and feared in equal measure across Europe.

Today the historic Fitzalan estate felt like the prison it was. If I was honest, it had never been a home.

My mother had died when I was barely eight, and in my memories of her she was always crying. I had been left to the tender mercies of Grand-Mère, before her death, and my father, who was forever disappointed in me, but still my only remaining parent.

And Celeste, who was ten years older than me. And better at everything.

Having lost my mother, I held fast to what was left of my family, and no matter if that grip often felt a good deal more like a choke hold I was performing on myself. They were all I had.

"You must look to your sister as your guide," Grand-Mère had told me on more than one occasion. Usually when I'd been discovered running in the corridors of the old house, disheveled and embarrassing, when I should have been sitting decorously somewhere, learning how to cross my ankles and incline my head in sweet subservience.

I had tried. I truly had.

I had watched Celeste come of age before me, elegant and meek in ways I envied and yet failed to understand. She had done it all with grace and beauty, the way she did everything. She had been married on her twentieth birthday to a man closer in age to our father—a hereditary count who claimed the blood of famed kings on both sides, stretching deep into Europe's gloried past. A man who I had never seen crack so much as the faintest smile.

And in the years since, Celeste had presented her ever-glowering husband with two sons and a daughter. Because while I had been raised to do my duty and knew what was expected of me—despite the dark thoughts I had about it in private while dreaming of Frederick's blue eyes—Celeste had *bloomed* in her role as countess.

It was hard to look at all that blooming, I thought uncharitably now. Not the day before I turned twenty-two, came into my fortune, and—not coincidentally, I was well aware—married the man of my father's choosing, who I had never met. My father felt a meeting was unnecessary and no one argued with Dermot Fitzalan, least of all the daughters he used as disposable pawns.

Happy birthday to me, I told myself darkly.

I would celebrate with a forced march down the aisle with a man whose very name made even the servants in the manor house recoil in horror.

A man I knew all manner of terrible things about.

A man widely regarded as a devil in the flesh.

A man who was not even the member of some or other gentry, as I had expected my eventual husband would be, given my father's celestially high opinion of himself and all he felt his vaunted pedigree—and thus mine—demanded.

In contrast, Celeste's husband, the dour count, had a title that ached with age—but had very few lands behind it. Or any money left over after all those centuries of aristocratic splendor, I had heard them whisper.

And this, I knew, was why my father had chosen a man for me who might have lacked gentility and pedigree, but more than made up for both with his astonishing wealth. Because this would surely add to the Fitzalan reach and financial might.

Genteel Celeste, so gentle and fragile, had been married carefully to a title that would sit well on her perfect brow. I was hardier. I could be sold off to a commoner whose coffers only seemed to swell by the year. In this way, my father could have his cake and eat it, merrily.

I knew this. But it didn't mean I liked it.

Celeste settled herself on the other end of the settee beneath the windows in my sitting room, where I had curled in a miserable ball this gray January day as if my brooding could make time stand still and save me from my fate.

"You will only make yourself ill," she told me, pragmatically. Or at least, that was how I interpreted the way she gazed at me then, down the length of the aristocratic nose she shared with our father. "And nothing will change either way. It is a wasted effort."

"I do not wish to marry him, Celeste."

Celeste let out that lilting laugh that I normally thought sounded like the finest music. Today it clawed at me.

"You do not *wish*?" She laughed again, and I wondered if I imagined the hardness in her gaze when it faded. "But who, pray, told you that your wishes mattered?"

I noted the year in as grim a tone as I could manage. "Surely my wishes should be consulted, at the very least. Even if nothing I want is taken into account."

"Fitzalans are not modern, Imogen," Celeste said with a hint of impatience, as I knew my father would. Though he would not *hint*. "If what you want is progress and self-determination, I'm afraid you were born into the wrong family."

"It was hardly my choice."

"Imogen. This is so childish. You have always known this day would come. You cannot possibly have imagined that *you*, somehow, would escape what waits for every Fitzalan from birth."

I turned that over and over in my head, noting it felt more bitter every time. More acrid.

The way she said *you*, with what sounded a great deal like scorn.

And the way she'd said *escape*, as if the very notion was fantastical.

It suggested she was neither as effortless nor as *joyfully blooming* as I had always imagined. And I didn't know quite how to process that possibility.

I shivered, here in these gloomy rooms built to impress fellow Norman invaders centuries ago en route to their sacking and pillaging of England, not to provide any semblance of comfort for the descendants of those invaders. I stared out the window at the deceptively quiet countryside spread out before me. The gardens that rolled this way and that, dead now, but still scrupulously maintained and manicured. I pretended I didn't know that the front of the house was decidedly less tranquil today as the family and guests gathered to cheer me on to my doom.

Celeste and her family in from Vienna, our shriveled great uncles from Paris, the impertinent cousins from Germany. My father's well-fed and sly business associates and rivals from all over the planet.

Not to mention the terrifying groom. The monster I was expected to marry in the morning.

"What is he like?" I asked, my voice cracking.

Celeste was quiet so long that I dragged my gaze from the window to study her expression.

I don't know what I expected. But it wasn't what I saw—my sister's mouth tilted up in the corners, like a cat in the cream.

An unpleasant jolt walloped me in the gut, then shivered through me. I endeavored to shake it off. Or better yet, ignore it.

"Are you sure you wish to know?" Celeste asked, after another long moment of nothing but that self-satisfied half smile that boded all manner of ill, I was sure. It shuddered through me like some kind of fear. "I am not certain that anything is gained by approaching an arranged marriage with an excess of knowledge about a man you must come to terms with, one way or another, no matter what you know ahead of time."

"You did not marry a monster," I retorted.

Though when I thought of the count and that expression of his that suggested he had never encountered a scent he did not abhor and never would, I wondered if the term *monster* might not have a variety of applications.

That smile of hers, if possible, grew ever more smug and made that shuddering thing in me all the more intense.

"He is not like anyone you have met, Imogen. It is impossible to prepare for the impact of him, really."

"I don't understand what that means."

Again, that tinkling laugh. "I must remind myself you are so young. Sheltered. Untouched, in every possible way."

"You were younger when you got married. And presumably, equally untouched and sheltered."

But the way she looked at me then made my heart stutter in my chest. Because if her sly, faintly pitying expression was to be believed, my half sister was not at all who I had believed her to be all this time.

And if Celeste was not Celeste…it was almost as if I forgot who I was, too.

The truth was, I didn't know what to make of it. I shoved it aside, thinking I'd take it out and look at it again when I could breathe normally again. Sometime in the dim future when I was married and settled and had somehow survived the monster who was already in this house, waiting for me.

"I feel sorry for you," Celeste murmured, after a moment, though her tone did not strike me as the sort one would use if that was true. "Truly, it isn't fair. How can a naive little thing like you be expected to handle a man like Javier Dos Santos?"

Even his name struck dread through the center of me. I told myself it had to be dread, that thick and too-hot sensation. It hit me in the chest, then spiraled down until it lodged itself low in my belly.

That, I told myself, was a measure of how much I loathed and feared him.

"I thought you hated him," I reminded my sister. "After what he did to you…"

I remembered the shouting. My father's deep voice echoing through the house. I remembered Celeste's sobs. Until now, it had been the only example I'd ever seen of something less than perfection in my half sister—and I had blamed the man who was the cause of it. I had held him responsible for the commotion. The jagged tear in the smooth inevitability that was our life here, so securely beneath our father's thumb.

More than this, I remembered the one glimpse I'd had of Javier Dos Santos in person. After another bout of screams and sobs and the sort of fighting I'd been taught Fitzalans were above, I had plastered myself to the window over the grand front entrance where I could hide myself in the drapery, and I had gazed down at this monster who had threatened to tear my family apart.

It had been years ago, but my memories remained as vivid as if it had happened yesterday.

He was dark like sin. A stain against the stones. His hair was glossy and black, so dark it looked nearly blue and reminded me of nothing so much as a raven's wing. His face was cruel and hard, so harsh it took my breath away. He had been made of muscle, hard and dangerous, a striking counterpoint to the genteel men I had been raised with. He was not elegant. He was not graceful.

He had no right to my beautiful sister, I had thought fiercely.

A sentiment my father had echoed in no uncertain terms. Celeste, he had bellowed throughout the manor house, was meant for better.

But it seemed Javier Dos Santos was good enough for me.

"Of course I do not hate him," Celeste said now, with more of that laughter that seemed to suggest I was very young and foolish. I didn't care for it, but I couldn't work out how to ask her to stop. "Where do you get such ideas?"

"From you. When you screamed that you hated him, and would hate him forever, and would never cheapen yourself by succumbing to the kind of dime-store forgiveness—"

"Here is what I can tell you about Javier," Celeste said, cutting me off. And pronouncing his name as if it was a meal. "He is not like other men. You should know this, going in. Throw out any preconceptions you might have."

"The only man I know is Father. A handful of priests. And your husband."

I had not meant to say those words the way I did. *Your husband.* As if I was pronouncing some kind of judgment.

But Celeste settled farther back against the settee as if she was relaxing. As if this was the moment she could finally retreat from her usual strict perfection and render herself boneless. "Javier is virile. Animal-istic, even. He will take what he wants, and worse, you will happily debase yourself to give it to him."

I frowned. "I have no intention of debasing myself. Much less happily."

Celeste waved a hand. "You will. He will demean you, insult you, and likely make you cry. And you will thank him for it."

My heart was pounding so hard it made me feel dizzy. My throat was dry, and my tongue felt thick in my mouth. And that dread seemed to pulse in me, hotter and wilder by the second.

"Why are you telling me these things? The day before I must marry him?"

If Celeste was abashed, she didn't look it. At all. "I am merely trying to prepare you, Imogen."

"I already think he is a monster. I'm not certain why you think talk of debasement and insults would improve the situation."

"You will have to watch that tongue of yours, of course," she said, almost sadly. "He won't put up with it. Or the way you run about heedlessly as if you are one of those common women on a treadmill somewhere, sweaty and red-faced."

Because she was naturally slim and beautiful, of course. She assumed that anyone who had to work for perfection didn't deserve it.

It had somehow never occurred to me before that this description might apply to me, too.

"You are very lucky, then, that you were spared this," I said softly. "That I am here to carry this burden for you. For the family."

I had never seen her look as she did then. Her face

flushed with what I could only call some kind of temper. Her chin rose. And her eyes glittered. "Indeed. I count myself lucky daily."

I found my hands on the hem of my pajama top, fiddling with the fine cotton as if I could worry it into threads. Betraying my anxiety, I knew.

And as strangely as my sister was behaving today, she was still my sister. The only person who had never punished me for asking questions.

This was why I dared to ask the one thing that had worried me the most since my father had announced my engagement to me over Christmas dinner.

"Do you think…?" I cleared my throat. "Will he hurt me?"

For a long moment, Celeste did not speak. And when she did, there was a hard look in her eyes, her lips twisted, and she no longer looked the least bit relaxed.

"You will survive it," she told me, something bleak and ugly there between us. "You will always survive it, Imogen, for better or worse, and that is what you will hold on to. My advice to you is to get pregnant as quickly as possible. Men like this want heirs. In the end, that is all they want. The sooner you do your duty, the quicker they will leave you alone."

And long after she swept from my room, I stayed where I was, stricken. And unable to breathe. There was a constriction in my chest and that heavy dread in my gut, and I couldn't help but think that I had seen my half sister—truly seen her—for the first time today.

It filled me like a kind of grief.

But I was also filled with a kind of restlessness I didn't understand.

That was what got me up and onto my feet. I dashed the odd moisture from my eyes with hands I knew better than to keep in fists. I started for the door, then imagined—too vividly—my father's reaction should I be found wandering about the house when it was filled with important wedding guests, clad only in my pajamas with my hair obviously unbrushed.

I went into my bedroom and dressed quickly, pulling on the dress the maids had left out for me, wordlessly encouraging me to clothe myself the way my father preferred. Not to my own taste, which would never have run to dresses at this chilly time of year, no matter that this one was long-sleeved and made of a fine wool. I paired the dress with butter-soft knee-high leather boots, and then found myself in my mirror.

I had not transformed into elegance during my vigil on the settee.

Curls like mine always looked unkempt. Elegance was sleek and smooth, but my hair resisted any and all attempts to tame it. The nuns had done what they could, but even they had been unable to combat my hair's natural tendency to find its own shape. I ran my fingers through it as best I could, letting the curls do as they would because they always did.

My hair was the bane of my existence. Much as I was the bane of my father's.

Only then, when I could say that in all honesty I had at least tried to sort myself out into something resembling order, did I leave my room.

I made my way out into the hall in the family wing, then ducked into one of the servants' back stairs. My father would not approve of his daughter moving about the house like one of the help, but I had never thought that he needed to know how familiar I was with the secret passages in this old pile of stones. Knowing them made life here that much more bearable.

Knowing my way through the shadows allowed me to remain at large when there was a lecture brewing. It permitted me to come in from long walks on the grounds, muddy and disheveled, and make it to my own rooms before the sight of me caused the usual offense, outrage, and threats to curtail my exercise until I learned how to behave *like a lady*.

I carefully made my way over to the guest wing, skirting around the rooms I knew had been set aside for various family members and my father's overfed friends. I knew that there was only one possible place my father would have dared put a man as wealthy and powerful as Javier Dos Santos. Only one place suitable for a groom with such a formidable financial reputation.

My father might have turned Javier from the house ten years ago, but now that he was welcome and set to marry the right daughter, Dermot Fitzalan would spare him no possible luxury.

I headed for what was one of the newer additions to the grand old house, a two-story dwelling place appended to the end of the guest wing where my grandmother had lived out her final days. It was more a house all its own, with its own entrance and rooms, but I knew that I could access it on the second level and sneak my way along its private gallery.

I didn't ask myself why I was doing this. I only knew it was tied to the grief I felt for the sister it turned out I barely knew and that dread inside me that pulsed at me, spurring me on.

I eased my way through the servant's door that disappeared behind a tapestry at one end of the gallery. I flattened myself to the wall and did my best to keep my ears peeled for any signs of life.

And it was the voice I heard first.

His voice.

Commanding. Dark. Rich like dark chocolate and deep red wine, all wrapped in one.

Beautiful, something in me whispered.

I was horrified with myself. But I didn't back away.

He was speaking in rapid Spanish, liquid and lovely, out of sight on the floor below me. I inched forward, moving away from the gallery wall so I could look over the open side of the balcony to the great room below.

And for a moment, memory and reality seemed tangled up in each other. Once again, I was gazing down at Javier Dos Santos from afar. From above.

Once again, I was struck by how *physical* he seemed. Long ago, he had been dressed for the evening in a coat with tails that had only accentuated the simmering brutality he seemed to hold leashed there in his broad shoulders and his granite rock of a torso.

Today he stood in a button-down shirt tucked into trousers that did things I hardly understood to his powerful thighs. I only knew I couldn't look away.

Once again, my heart beat so hard and so fast I was worried I might be ill.

But I wasn't.

I knew I wasn't.

I watched him rake his fingers through that dark hair of his, as black and as glossy as I remembered it, as if even the years dared not defy him. He listened to the mobile he held at one ear for a moment, his head cocked to one side, then replied in another spate of the lyrical Spanish that seem to wind its way around me. Through me. Deep inside me, too.

With my functional Spanish I could pick up the sense of the words, if not every nuance. Business concerns in Wales. Something about the States. And a fiercer debate by far about Japan.

He finished his call abruptly, then tossed his mobile onto the table next to him. It thunked against the hard wood, making me too aware of the silence.

And too conscious of my own breathing and my mad, clattering heart.

Javier Dos Santos stood there a moment, his attention on the papers before him, or possibly his tablet computer.

When he raised his head, he did it swiftly. His dark eyes were fierce and sure, pinning me where I stood. I understood in a sudden red haze of exposure and fear that he had known I was here all along.

He had known.

"Hello, Imogen," he said, switching to faintly accented English that made my name sound like some kind of incantation. Or terrible curse. "Do you plan to do something more than stare?"

CHAPTER TWO

Javier

I WAS A man built from lies.

My faithless father. My weak, codependent mother. The lies they had told—to each other, to the world, to me and my sisters—had made me the man I was today, for good or ill.

I allowed no room in the life I had crafted from nothing for lies like theirs. Not from my employees or associates. Not from my sisters, grown now and beholden to me. Not from a single soul on this earth.

And certainly not from myself.

So there was no hiding from the fact that my first glimpse of my future bride—the unfortunate Fitzalan sister, as she was known—did not strike me the way I had anticipated it would.

I had expected that she would do well enough. She was not Celeste, but she was a Fitzalan. It was her pedigree that mattered, that and the sweet, long-anticipated revenge of forcing her father to give me the very thing he had denied me once already.

I had never done well with denial. Ten years ago it had not taken me to my knees, as I suspected Dermot Fitzalan thought it would. On the contrary, it had led me to go bigger, to strive harder, to make absolutely certain that the next time I came for a Fitzalan daughter, their arrogant, self-satisfied father would not dare deny me.

I had expected that my return to this cold, gloomy mausoleum in the north of France would feel like a victory lap. Because it was.

What I did not expect was the kick of lust that slammed through me at the sight of her.

It made no sense. I had been raised in the gutters of Madrid, but I had always wanted better. Always. As I'd fought my way out of the circumstances of my birth, I'd coveted elegance and collected it wherever I could.

It had made sense for me to pursue Celeste. She was grace personified, elegant from the tips of her fingernails to the line of her neck, and nothing but ice straight through.

It had made sense that I had wanted her to adorn my collection.

The girl before me, who had dared try to sneak up on a man who had been raised in dire pits filled with snakes and jackals and now walked untroubled through packs of wolves dressed as aristocrats, was…unruly.

She had red-gold hair that slithered this way and that and stubborn curls she had made no apparent attempt to tame. There was a spray of freckles over her nose, and I knew that if I could see them from this distance, it likely meant that my eyes were not deceiving me and she had not, in fact, bothered with even the faintest hint of cosmetics in a nod toward civility.

On the one hand, that meant her dark, thick lashes and the berry shade of her full lips were deliciously natural.

But it also showed that she had little to no sense of propriety.

She was otherwise unadorned. She wore a navy blue dress that was unobjectionable enough, with classic lines that nodded toward her generous figure without making too much of it, and leather boots that covered her to her knees.

I could have forgiven the hair and even the lack of cosmetics—which suggested she had not prepared for her first meeting with me the way a woman who planned to make the perfect wife would have.

But it was the way she was scowling at me that suggested she was even less like her sister than I had imagined.

Celeste had never cracked. Not even when she'd been denied what she'd so prettily claimed she wanted. Oh, she'd caused a carefully prepared scene for her father, but there had never been anything but calculation in her gaze. Her mascara had never run. She had never presented anything but perfection, even in the midst of her performance.

The fact it still rankled made it a weakness. I thrust it aside.

"Surely that is not the expression you wish to show your future husband," I said quietly. "On this, the occasion of our first meeting."

I had heard her come in and creep along the strange balcony above me the butler had told me was a gallery. Not a very good gallery, I had thought with a derisive glance at the art displayed there. All stodgy old masters and boring ecclesiastical works. Nothing bold. Nothing new.

Until she'd come.

"I want to know why you wish to marry me." She belted that out, belligerent and bordering on rude. A glance confirmed that she was making fists at her sides. *Fists*.

I felt my brow raise. "I beg your pardon?"

Her scowl deepened. "I want to know why you want to marry me, when if you are even half as rich and powerful as they say, you could marry anyone."

I thrust my hands—not in anything resembling fists—into the pockets of my trousers, and considered her.

I should have been outraged. I told myself I was.

But the truth was, there was something about her that tempted me to smile. And I was not a man who smiled easily, if at all.

I told myself it was the very fact that she had come here, when our wedding was not until the morning. It was the fact she seemed to imagine she could put herself between her grasping, snobbish father and me when these were matters that could not possibly concern her. Daughters of men like Dermot Fitzalan always did what they were told, sooner or later.

Yet here she was.

It was the futility of it, I thought. My Don Quixote bride with her wild hair, tilting at windmills and scowling all the while. It made something in my chest tighten.

"I will answer any questions you have," I told her magnanimously, trying my best to contain my own ferocity. "But you must face me."

"I'm looking right at you."

I only raised a hand, then beckoned her to me with two languid fingers.

And then waited, aware that it had been a long time indeed since I had been in the presence of someone…unpredictable.

I saw her hands open, then close again at her sides. I saw the way her chest moved, telling me that she fought to keep her breath even.

I learned a lot about my future bride as the seconds ticked by, and all she did was stare down at me. I learned she was willful. Defiant.

But ultimately yielding.

Because when she moved, it was to the spiral stair that led her down to the stone floor where I stood.

Perhaps not yielding so much as curious, I amended as she drew near, folding her arms over her chest as if she was drawing armor around herself in order to face me.

I took a moment to consider her, this bride I had purchased outright. This girl who was my revenge and my prize, all in one.

She will do, I thought, pleased with myself.

"I suppose," I said after a moment, in the cool tone I used to reprimand my subordinates, "you cannot help the hair."

Imogen glowered at me. Her eyes were an unusual shade of brown that looked like old copper coins when they filled with temper, as they did now. It made me wonder how they would look when she was wild with passion instead.

That lust hit me again. Harder this time.

"It is much like being born without a title, I imagine," she retorted.

It took me a moment to process that. To understand that this messy, unruly girl had thrust such an old knife in so deftly, then twisted it.

I couldn't think of the last time that had happened. I couldn't think of the last person who had dared.

"Does it distress you that you must lower yourself to marry a man so far beneath you?" I asked, all silk and threat. "A man who is little more than a mongrel while you have been deliberately bred from blood kept blue enough to burn?"

I could not seem to help but notice that her skin was so fair it was like cream and made me...hungry. And when her eyes glittered, they gleamed copper.

"Does it distress you that I am not my sister?" she asked in return.

I hadn't expected that.

I felt myself move, only dimly aware that I was squaring my shoulders and changing my stance, as if I found myself engaged in hand-to-hand combat. I supposed I was.

"You cannot imagine that the two of you could be confused," I murmured, but I was looking at her differently. I was viewing her as less a pawn and more an opponent. First a knife, then a sucker punch.

So far, Imogen Fitzalan was proving to be far more interesting that I had anticipated.

I wasn't sure I knew where to put that.

"As far as I am aware," she said coolly, "you are the only one who has ever confused us."

"I assure you, I am not confused."

"Perhaps I am. I assume that purchasing my hand in marriage requires at least as much research as the average online dating profile. Did you not see a picture? Were you not made aware that my sister and I share only half our blood?"

"I cannot say I gave the matter of your appearance much thought," I said, and I expected that to set her back on her heels.

But instead, the odd creature laughed.

"A man like you, not concerned with his own wife's appearance? How out of character."

"I cannot imagine what you think you know of my character."

"I have drawn conclusions about your character based on the way you allow yourself to be photographed." Her brow lifted. "You are a man who prefers the company of a very particular shape of woman."

"It is not their shape that concerns me, but whether or not other men covet them." This was nothing but the truth, and yet something about the words seemed almost…oily. Weighted. As if I should be ashamed of saying such a thing out loud when I had said it many times before.

Though not, I amended, to a woman I intended to make my wife.

"You like a trophy," she said.

I inclined my head. "I am a collector, Imogen. I like only the finest things."

She smiled at me, but it struck me as more of a baring of teeth. "You must be disappointed indeed."

Though she looked as if the notion pleased her.

I moved then, closer to her, enjoying the way she stood fast instead of shrinking away. I could see the way her pulse beat too fast in her neck. I could see the way her copper eyes widened. I reached over and helped myself to one of those red-gold curls, expecting her hair to be coarse. Much as she was.

But the curl was silky against my fingers, sliding over my skin like a caress. And something about that fell through me like a sudden brush fire.

If I was a man who engaged in self-deception, I would have told myself that was not at all what I felt.

But I had built my life and my fortune, step by impossible step in the face of only overwhelming odds, on nothing short of brutal honesty. Toward myself and others, no matter the cost.

I knew I wanted her.

She reached up as if to bat my hand away, but appeared to think better of it, which raised her another notch or two in my estimation. "You have yet to answer the question. You can marry anyone you like. Why on earth would you choose me?"

"Perhaps I am so enamored of the Fitzalan name that I have hungered for nothing but the opportunity to align myself with your father since the day I met your sister. And you should know, Imogen, that I always get what I want."

She swallowed. I watched the pale column of her neck move when she did. "They say you are a monster."

I was so busy looking at her mouth and imagining how those plump lips would feel wrapped around the hungriest part of me that I almost missed the way she said that. And more, the look on her face when she did.

As if she was not playing a game, any longer.

As if she was actually afraid of me.

And I had dedicated my life to making certain that as many people as possible were afraid of me, because a healthy fear bred respect and I did not much care if they feared me so long as they respected me.

But somehow, I did not wish this to be true of Imogen Fitzalan. My bride, for her sins.

"Those who say I am a monster are usually poor losers," I told her, aware that I was too close to her. And yet neither she nor I moved to put more space between us. "It is in their best interests to call me a monster, because who could be expected to prevail against a creature of myth and lore? Their own shortcomings and failures are of no consequence, you understand. Not if I am a monster instead of a man."

Her gaze searched my face. "You want to be a monster, then. You enjoy it."

"You can call me whatever you like. I will marry you all the same."

"Again. Why me?"

"Why does this upset you?" I didn't fight the urge that came over me then, to reach over and take her chin in my fingers and hold her face where I wanted it. Simply because I could. And because, though she stilled, she did not jerk away. "I know that you have spent your life preparing for this day. Why should it matter if it is me or anyone else?"

"It matters."

Her voice was fierce and quiet at once. And emotion gleamed in her lovely eyes, though I couldn't discern what, exactly, that sheen meant.

"Did you have your heart set on another?" I asked, aware as I did so that something I had never felt before stirred to life within me. "Is that why you dare come to me with all this belligerence?"

It was because she was mine, I told myself. That was why I felt that uncharacteristic surge of possessiveness. I had not felt it for a woman before, it was true. Despite how much I had wanted Celeste back in the day and how infuriated I had been when I had lost her to that aristocratic zombie of a count she called her husband.

I had wanted Celeste, yes.

But that was a different thing entirely than knowing she was meant to be mine.

Imogen was mine. There was no argument. I had paid for the privilege—or that was how her father planned to spin this match.

He and I knew the truth. I was a wealthy man, my power and might with few equals. I took care of my sisters and my mother because I prided myself on my honor and did my duty—not because they deserved that consideration. And because I did not want them to be weak links others could use to attack me.

But otherwise I had no ties or obligations, and had thus spent my days dedicating myself to the art of money.

The reality was that Dermot Fitzalan needed my wealth. And better still, my ability to make more with seeming ease. He needed these things far more than I needed his daughter's pedigree.

But I had decided long ago that I would marry a Fitzalan heiress, these daughters of men who had been the power behind every throne in Europe at one point or another. I had determined that I would make my babies on soft, well-bred thighs, fatten them on blue blood, and raise them not just rich, but cultured.

I had been so young when I had seen Celeste that first time. So raw and unformed. The animal they accused me of being in all the ways that mattered.

I had never seen a woman like her before. All clean lines and beauty. I had never imagined that a person could be…flawless.

It had taken me far longer than it should have—far longer than it would today, that was for certain—to see the truth of Celeste Fitzalan, now a countess of petty dreams and an angry old man's promises because that was what she had wanted far more than she had wanted me.

But my thirst for my legacy had only grown stronger.

"If there was another," my confounding betrothed said, a mulish set to that fine mouth and a rebellion in her gaze, "I would hardly be likely to tell you, would I?"

"You can tell me anything you like about others," I told her, all menace and steel. "Today. I would advise you to take advantage of this offer. Come the morning, I will take a far dimmer view of these things."

"It doesn't matter what I want," she threw at me, pulling her chin from my grasp.

I assumed we were both well aware that I allowed it.

"I never said that it did. You are the one who came here. Was it only to call me names? To ask me impertinent questions? Or perhaps you had another goal in mind?"

"I don't know why I came," Imogen said, and I could tell by the way her voice scraped into the air between us that she meant that.

But there was a fire in me. A need, dark and demanding, and I was not in the habit of denying myself the things I wanted.

More than this, she was to be my wife in the morning.

"Don't worry," I told her with all that heat and intent. "I know exactly why you came."

I hooked my hand around her neck, enjoying the heat of her skin beneath the cover of those wild curls. I pulled her toward me, watching her eyes go wide and her mouth drop open as if she couldn't help herself. As if she was that artless, that innocent.

I couldn't understand the things that worked in me. To take her, to possess her, to bury myself in her body when she looked nothing like the women that I usually amused myself with.

But none of that mattered.

Because I already owned her. All that remained was the claiming, and I wanted it. Desperately.

I dropped my mouth to hers.

CHAPTER THREE

Imogen

HE WAS KISSING ME.

The monster was kissing me.

And I hardly knew what to do.

His mouth was a bruising thing, powerful and hard. It should have hurt, surely. I should have wanted nothing more than to get away from all that intensity. I should have tried. But instead, I found myself pushing up on my toes and leaning toward him…

As if I wanted more.

He cradled the back of my head in one hand and moved his lips over mine.

And I *wanted*. I wanted…everything.

I had dreamed of kisses half my life. I had longed for a moment like this. A punishing kiss, perhaps. Or something sweet and filled with wonder. Any kind of kiss at all, if I was honest.

But nothing could have prepared me for Javier Dos Santos.

Nothing could have prepared me for this.

I felt his tongue against the seam of my lips, and couldn't help myself from opening up and giving him entry. And then I thought I would give him anything.

And even though I understood, on some distant level, what he was doing to me—that his tongue was testing mine, dancing here, then retreating— all I could feel was the heat. *The heat*. Something greedy and wild and impossibly hot, thrilling to life inside me. What I had called dread had melted into something else entirely, something molten. It wound around and around inside my chest, knotted up in my belly, and dripped like honey even lower.

And still he kissed me.

His arms were a marvel. Heavy and hard, they wrapped around me, making me feel things I could hardly understand. Small, yet safe. Entirely surrounded, yet sweet, somehow.

Still Javier's mouth moved on mine. He bent me backward, over one strong arm. His heavy chest, all steel planes and granite, pressed hard against mine, until I felt my breasts seem to swell in response.

It was like a fever.

The ache was everywhere, prickling and hot, but I knew—somehow I knew—I wasn't ill.

He bent me back even farther and there was a glory in it. I felt weightless, too caught up in all that fire and honey to worry whether or not my feet still touched the ground.

And then I felt his fingers as they found their way beneath the hem of my dress, a scandalous caress that made my heart stutter. Yet he didn't stop. He tracked that same sweet flame along the length of my thigh, climbing ever higher.

My brain shorted out. The world went white-hot, then red-hot, then it became nothing at all but need.

His hand was a wonder. Not soft and manicured, like the hands of the very few men whose hands I'd shaken at some point or other, but hard and calloused. Big, and brutally masculine.

He traced some kind of pattern into my skin, and then laughed against my mouth when I shuddered in response.

His taste was like wine. It washed through me in the same way, leaving me flushed, giddy.

And then his fingers toyed with the edge of my panties, until I was sure I stopped breathing.

Not that I cared when he angled his head, taking the kiss deeper. Hotter.

While at the same time, his fingers moved with bold certainty to find my soft heat.

And then, to my wonder and shame, he began to stroke me, there below.

His tongue was in my mouth. His fingers were deep between my legs, and I couldn't remember why I had ever thought this man was a monster. Or maybe

I thought he was a far greater monster than I'd ever imagined.

Either way, I surrendered. And my surrender felt like strength.

It was like some kind of dance. Parry, then retreat. His mouth and his hand, one and then the other, or both at once.

Before I knew it, that fever in me was spreading. I shook, everywhere. I could feel my own body grow stiff in his arms and I felt myself edging ever closer to crisis.

I would have pushed him away if I could. If I could make my hands do anything but grip the front of his shirt as I shook and stiffened and spun further and further off into that blazing need.

I lost myself somewhere between Javier's hot, hard mouth and his pitiless hand between my legs. I lost myself, and I followed that shaking, and I hardly understood why I was making those greedy, shameful noises in the back of my throat—

"Come apart for me, Imogen," he growled against my mouth, as if he owned even this. "Now."

And there was nothing in me but heat and surrender.

I exploded on cue.

And I was only dimly aware of it when Javier set me away from him. He settled me on the lip of the table behind us, ran his hands down my arms as if he was reminding me of the limits of my own body, and even smoothed the skirt of my dress back into place.

I was tempted to find it all sweet, however strange a word that seemed when applied to a man so widely regarded as a monster. A man I still thought of in those terms. But there was a tumult inside of me.

My head spun and everything inside me followed suit. I couldn't focus. I couldn't breathe. I couldn't make sense of what had happened.

And when my breathing finally slowed enough that I could think beyond it, Javier was waiting there. He stood in the same position he'd been standing before, his hands thrust into the pockets of the trousers I knew at a glance had been crafted by hand in an atelier in a place like Milan or Paris.

His might seemed more overwhelming now. I had a vague memory of the stable boy's dreamy blue eyes, but they seemed so insubstantial next to Javier's relentless masculinity. I felt it like a storm. It buffeted me, battering my skin, until I felt the electricity of it—of him—as if he had left some part of himself inside me.

I told myself I hated him for it.

"You look upset, *mi reina*," Javier murmured. I understood the words he used—Spanish for *my queen*—but stiffened at the dark current of mockery in it. "Surely not. I am certain someone must have prepared you for what goes on between a man and a woman no matter how hard your father has worked to keep you locked up in a tower."

I was not one of the sacrificial maidens ransomed out of this place in centuries past, despite appearances. I might have lived a sheltered life, but that life came with abundant internet access.

Still, I followed an urge inside of me, a dark insistence I didn't have it in me to resist.

"I prepared in the usual way," I told him. "Locked towers might work in fairy tales. They are harder to manage in real life, I think."

And when his dark gaze turned to fire and burned where it touched me, I only held it. And practiced that half smile I had seen on my sister's face earlier.

"I will assume you mean that your preparation for marriage took place under the careful tutelage of disinterested nuns as they discussed biology."

I channeled Celeste. "Assume what you like."

Right there, before my eyes, Javier…changed. I had thought he was stone before, but he became something harder. Flint and granite, straight through.

I couldn't tell if the pulse that pounded in me then—in my wrists and my ears, my breasts and between my legs—was fear or something else. Something far more dangerous.

All I knew was that I wanted whatever Celeste had appeared to have on my settee. I wanted that confidence. I even wanted her smugness.

Because it seemed to me that was some measure of power.

I didn't want to be what they called me. The lesser Fitzalan sister. The unfortunate one. Not here. Not now.

I didn't want this man—who had broken me wide-open in ways I didn't know how to explain without, as far as I could tell, so much as breaking a sweat— to know how inexperienced I was. I didn't want to give him my innocence, particularly if he thought it was his by right.

Just once, I thought defiantly, I wanted to feel sophisticated.

Just once, I wanted to be the sleek one, the grace-ful one.

I wasn't sure I could fake my sister's effortless-ness. But I knew that my smirk was getting to him. I could see it in all that stone and metal that made his face so harsh.

"All the better," Javier growled at me, though he didn't look anything like pleased. "You should know that I am a man of a great many needs, Imogen. That I will not have to tutor you how best to meet them can only be a boon."

I didn't believe him. I didn't know what it was that whispered to me that he minded a great deal more than he was saying, but I knew it all the same.

Or you want *to know it*, something whispered in me, leaving marks. *You want to affect him, somehow, after he took your breath away like this.*

I didn't want to think such things. I found myself frowning at him instead.

"Careful," Javier said with a soft menace that made me feel molten and shivery all over again. "If you do not want an example of the sort of appetites I mean, here and now, I'd suggest you go back wherever you came from. There is a wedding in the morning. And an entire marriage before us in which, I promise you, you will have ample time to learn what it is I want and expect. In bed and out."

And then I felt twisted. As if there was something wrong deep within me. Because the fact he was dismissing me stung, when I knew I should have been grateful for the reprieve. I flushed again, but this time it felt more like poison than that same impossible, irresistible heat.

I was only pretending to be like Celeste—and the look on Javier's harsh face suggested that I wasn't doing a particularly good job. I was certain that if he touched me again, I would never be able to keep it up.

And no matter that there was a part of me that shimmered with longing. That wanted nothing more than to feel his hands on me again. And more.

So much more.

I knew I had to take the escape hatch he had offered me—or lose myself even further.

Possibly even lose myself for good.

I slid off the table to find my feet, and fought to keep my expression from betraying how tender I felt where his hand had been between my legs. It felt as if my panties were somehow too tight, as if I was swollen, and I hardly knew how to walk on my own.

Yet I did. I managed it.

I skirted around him as if he was on fire, convinced that I could feel that blistering heat of his from feet away. Convinced that he had branded me, somehow. And entirely too aware of his glittering, arrogant gaze.

But I had a long night ahead of me to fret over such things.

I only understood that I expected him to reach out and take hold of me again when he didn't. And when I made it to the spiral stair and ran up it as fast as I could on my rubbery legs, the clatter of my heart inside my chest was so loud I was surprised he didn't hear it and comment on it from below.

I made my way along the second-floor gallery, aware of his gaze on me like a heavy weight—or some kind of chain binding me to him already—but I didn't turn back. I didn't dare look back.

Maybe there was a part of me that feared if I did, I might go to him again. That I would sink into that fire of his and burn alive, until there was nothing left of me but ashes.

When I slipped back beneath the tapestry and into the servants' walkway, there was no relief. It was like I carried Javier with me, in all the places he had touched me and, worse by far, all the places I only wished he had.

It was as if I was already half-consumed by that fire of his I both feared and longed for.

But I would die before I let him know that he had taught me more in those wild, hot moments than I had learned in a lifetime.

The reality was, I thought about what a wedding

night with this man might entail and I…thought I might die, full stop.

I knew that was melodramatic, but I indulged in it anyway as I made my way through the shadowy recesses of my father's house. Why had I gone to Javier in the first place? Why had I been so foolish? What had I imagined might happen? I wanted to sink into a bath and wash it all away, let the water soothe me and hide me. I simply wanted to be back in my rooms again, safe and protected.

Because a deep, feminine wisdom I hadn't known resided there inside me whispered these final hours before my wedding might be the last bit of safety I would know.

I knew too much now, and none of it things I'd wanted to learn. I had found a magic and a fire, yes. But now I knew how easily I surrendered. I knew how my body betrayed me.

I knew, worst of all, that I wanted things I was terribly afraid only Javier Dos Santos could give me.

And I wasn't paying sufficient attention when I slipped out from the servants' hall. I was usually far more careful. I usually listened for a good few minutes, then used the carefully placed eyeholes to be certain that no one was in sight before I slipped back into the house's main corridors.

But Javier had done something to me. He had used my own body against me, as if he knew what it could do better than I did. He had made me feel as if I belonged to him instead of to myself. Even with all this distance between us, clear on the other side of the rambling old manor house, I could feel his hands on me. Those powerful arms closed around me. His harsh, cruel mouth while it mastered mine.

That was the only excuse I could think of when I stepped out and found myself face-to-face with my father.

For a long, terrible moment, there was nothing but silence between us and the far-off sound of rain against the roof.

Dermot Fitzalan was neither tall nor particularly physically imposing, but he made up for both with the scorn he held for literally every person alive who was not him.

To say nothing of the extra helping he kept in reserve for me.

"Pray tell me that I have taken leave of my senses." His voice was so cold it made the ancient stone house feel balmy in comparison. I felt goose bumps prickle to life down my arms. "I beg you, Imogen—tell me that I did not witness an heiress to the Fitzalan fortune emerge from the servants' quarters like an inept housemaid I would happily dismiss on the spot."

I had imagined myself brave, before. When I had taken off on a whim and found the man my father had chosen for me. When I had tangled with a monster and walked away—changed, perhaps, but whole.

But I realized as I stood there, the focus of my father's withering scorn as I so often was, that when it counted I wasn't the least bit brave at all.

"I thought I heard a noise," I lied, desperately. "I only ducked my head in to see what it was."

"I beg your pardon." My father looked at me the way he always did, as if the sight of me was vaguely repulsive. "Why should a lady of this house, a daughter of the Fitzalan line, feel it is incumbent upon her to investigate strange noises? Are you unable to ring for assistance?"

"Father—"

He lifted a hand. That was all.

But that was all that was needed. It silenced me as surely as if he'd wrapped that hand around my throat and squeezed. The hard light in his dark gaze suggested it was not outside the realm of possibility.

"You are an enduring disappointment to me, Imogen." His voice was cold. Detached. And I already knew this to be so. There was no reason it should have felt like an unexpected slap when he took every opportunity to remind me how often and comprehensively I let him down. And yet my cheeks stung red as if he'd actually struck. "I do not understand this...willfulness."

He meant my hair. He meant those curls that had never obeyed anyone. Not him and not me, certainly. Not the relentless nuns, not my old governesses, not the poor maids he hired to attack me with their formulas and their straight irons to no avail.

"You might almost be pretty, if distressingly rough around the edges, were it not for that mess you insist on flaunting."

My father glared at my curls with such ferocity that I was almost surprised he didn't reach out and try to tear them off with his hand.

"I can't help my hair, Father," I dared to say in a low voice.

It was a mistake.

That ferocious glare left my hair and settled on me. Hard.

"Let me make certain you are aware of how I expect this weekend to go," he said, his voice lowering in that way of his that made my stomach drop. "In less than twenty-four hours you will be another man's problem. He will be forced to handle these pointless rebellions of yours, and I wish him good luck. But you will exit this house, and my protection, as befits a Fitzalan."

I didn't need to know what, specifically, he meant by that. What I knew about my father was that whenever he began to rant on about the things that *befit* a member of this family, it always ended badly for me.

Still, I wasn't the same girl who had foolishly wandered off in search of my husband-to-be. I wasn't the silly creature who had sat on my own settee staring out at the rain and dreaming of a stable boy. She felt far away to me now, a dream I had once had.

Because Javier Dos Santos had branded me as surely as if he'd pressed hot iron against my skin, and I could still feel the shock of it. The burn.

"What do you suggest I do?" I asked, with the

sort of spirit I knew my father would find offensive. I couldn't seem to help myself. "Shave it all off?"

My father bared his teeth and I shrank back, but it was no use. My back came up hard against the wall. There was nowhere for me to go.

And in any event, it was worse if I ran.

"I suspect you are well aware that I wish no such thing, Imogen." If possible, my father's voice dripped with further disdain. "I take it you imagine that your marriage will provide you with some measure of freedom. Perhaps you view it as an escape. If you know what is good for you, girl, you will readjust that attitude before tomorrow morning. Your new husband might not be of the blood, but I assure you, he expects total and complete obedience in all things."

"I never said—" I began.

My father actually smiled. It was chilling. "In fact, Dos Santos is nothing but a common, rutting creature who handles any and all conflict with the deftness you might expect from an uncivilized beast. I shudder to think how he will choose to handle these displays of yours."

I thought I had a good idea of how he might handle them now, but I dropped my gaze, terrified that my father might see all that need and fire Javier had taught me, written all over me. And because I didn't want to see the malicious glee I knew would be stamped all over my only living parent at the notion my husband would *handle* me.

I tried not to miss my mother as it did no good.

But in moments like this I couldn't help myself. I knew that if she'd lived, she wouldn't have defied my father, either, but at least I'd had no doubt she loved me.

"Silence at last?" my father taunted me. "That will not help you, either. The die is cast, I am afraid. You will spend the rest of this day and evening locked in your rooms. But do not imagine you will have the opportunity to retreat into those books you love so much, unnatural as you are. I will send in your attendants and mark my words, Imogen. I do not care if it takes from now until the moment the ceremony begins tomorrow, but you will look like a proper Fitzalan for the first time in your life, I swear it. You will tame that mess you call hair. You will do something with your face, for a change. You will be manicured and pedicured and forced to look like the pride and joy of this house no matter what it takes."

"Father," I tried again, "none of this is necessary."

"You cannot be trusted," he seethed at me. "You are an embarrassment. I have never understood how a child of my loins could come out so slovenly. Quite apart from those curls, look at how you walk around my house knowing full well we have important guests who expect the Fitzalan name to connote nothing but grace and elegance, handed down over centuries." His scornful glare swept me from forehead to toes, then back again. "You look as common as he is."

That was the worst insult my father could think to hurl at me.

And the part of me that wished I could please him, no matter how well I knew that was an impossibility, recoiled.

But I didn't say a word. I stood there, letting him skewer me in every way possible, because it wasn't as if there was any way to stop him. There never had been.

When he was done, he straightened, though he already stood as if there was an iron pole where his spine should have been. He adjusted the cuffs of his jacket indignantly, as if my slovenliness was contagious.

"Go to your rooms at once," he told me, as if I was a small child. Which was how I felt when he looked at me. "You will sit there and you will await your attendants."

"Yes, Father." I tried to sound obliging and obedient.

He reached over and grabbed my arm, his fingers closing painfully over my biceps. But I knew better than to make any sound of protest.

"You have less than a day remaining in this house," he hissed. "Less than a day remaining to conduct yourself appropriately. And I warn you, Imogen. If you attempt to embarrass me further, you will not like how this wedding ceremony goes. Remember that all I require is your presence at the ceremony. It is utterly irrelevant to me if you are capable of speaking or even standing."

He left me there, marching off without so much as a backward glance, because he was certain that I would obey him. He was certain—and he was right.

I knew that none of his threats were idle. He would roll me into my own wedding ceremony strapped down to a stretcher if he wished, and not one guest would raise an eyebrow. I wasn't a person to them. I wasn't *me*. I was a Fitzalan heiress, nothing more and nothing less, and it was my father's right to do with me what he pleased. The guests here were as interested in my feelings on what happened in my life as they would be in the thoughts of any piece of livestock.

I could feel the fingerprints Father had left on me, bruising up on my arm already. I ducked my head down, frustration and fury making my eyes water, as I headed toward my rooms.

As ordered.

But the things my father had said to me had, perhaps, the opposite effect of what he'd intended.

Because I had been so focused on Javier. On the fact he was meant to be a monster. I had been so worried about marching myself down the aisle and straight on into my own doom.

I hadn't spent nearly enough time thinking about the fact that monster or not, Javier could only be an improvement on the monster I would be leaving behind.

I might never be free, but I would be free of my father.

And if the price of that was an unpleasant evening of attempts to beat me into submission and make of me the perfect Fitzalan bride to honor my father's vanity, I could only believe it was worth it.

CHAPTER FOUR

Javier

I WASN'T ENTIRELY surprised that my blushing bride was nowhere to be seen at the tedious drinks affair Dermot Fitzalan threw that night.

After all, this was not the kind of wedding that got written up in the gossip pages or excessively photographed for the Style sections of various magazines across the globe, rife with planned events and excessive opportunities to celebrate the romantic idiocy of the marrying couple. My wedding was not a performance.

It was a contract and Imogen was incidental. I had paid for access. For a connection to the kings across time who lived in the Fitzalan name. For the pièce de résistance to add to my collection.

"Have you come with no family of your own, Dos Santos?" asked one of the wolves gathered for this occasion that I doubted anyone would call joyous. He was an overly titled idiot who had spent the last few moments risking his continuing health by standing too close to me and making a great show of looking around the room while he did it. He had obviously wished me to ask what he was doing. I had not. "What kind of man attends his own wedding solo?"

I raised my glass, but made no attempt to wrestle my expression into anything approaching polite. "A man who is well aware that he is making a business acquisition, which I am perfectly capable of doing without an entourage."

The other man brayed with laughter, and I was already bored. I left him without another word, making my way through the high-ceilinged room that had been set up to host this supposedly genial cocktail hour ahead of what promised to be an even duller banquet. I knew Fitzalan was showing off, the way he always did. The guests were meant to be in awe of this historical monument he called a house, me most of all. I was meant to be cowed into reverence by the medieval flourishes and the history in every ostentatious antique.

I was meant to feel small.

Sadly for Fitzalan and his self-regard, I felt quite the opposite.

I couldn't get my bride-to-be and her wild, wholly irreverent red-gold curls out of my head.

Imogen Fitzalan was not at all what I had been expecting and I could not recall the last time anything had surprised me. Much less a woman. Women tended to blur together for me, in truth. Those who approached me hungered for my wealth, my power, and were willing to trade their bodies for a taste of it. And who was I to refuse these generous offers? I accepted them, I enjoyed them, and then I promptly forgot them.

I had always known that I intended to marry a woman who could give my children the only thing I could not buy for them myself: blue blood.

But until that day came, I had always been perfectly happy to revel in the demands of the common red blood that coursed freely in me. It was a heavy pulse in me even now, surrounded by the pale blue aristocrats on all sides and the sort of ancient, theatrical objects cluttering every surface that I knew were meant to trumpet the value of their owner. I was surrounded by the worst sort of wolves, yet I was thinking about sex. All thanks to the bride I had expected would be a cold, prim virgin unable to make eye contact.

I wasn't sure what to do with the surprise I felt. I wasn't sure I liked it.

I made my way to the windows that overlooked the gloomy gardens out back as the fog rolled in to cap off another miserable French day. I preferred the bright heat of Spain, the warmth of my people, and the rhythm of my native language. I nursed my drink as I watched some of Europe's wealthiest men circle each other warily as if violence might erupt at any moment, when I knew very well that was not how men like these attacked. They preferred a stealthier approach. They came at their enemies through hostile takeovers and cruel buyouts. They wielded their fortunes like the armies of lesser men.

They didn't scare me. Not one of the men in this room had created what was his with his own hands. I was the only one here with that distinction.

It meant I was the only one here who knew what it was to live without these privileges. To grow up hard and have nothing but myself to rely on.

And that meant they had a weakness, a blindness, that I did not.

I was smiling at that notion when Celeste swept into the room on the arm of the animated corpse who had made her a countess. The decrepit aristocrat she had chosen over me.

I waited for that kick that I recalled so well at the sight of her. I had called it lust, back then. Lust and fury, need and madness.

But I knew it better now. Or I knew myself. It had been a kind of covetousness, the way I lusted after the finest cars and the most luxurious residences in the best locations. I had wanted Celeste, desperately. I had imagined she would be the crown jewel of my collection.

Yet tonight, as I saw her operate the room like the shark I hadn't realized she was ten years ago— despite that flat gaze and the smile she leveraged like a weapon—that kick was missing. Was it that I was a decade older now? Perhaps I had seen too much to be turned around by a gracefully inclined neck and too many pretty lies. Or was it that I had finally tasted something sweet today and wanted more of it instead of these bitter dregs of once proud family lines?

If they are bitter dregs, what are you? a harsh voice inside me asked. *As you are here to drink deep of what little they have to offer.*

I didn't know the answer. What I did know was that this evening wearied me already. It could have been any night on any continent in any city, surrounded by the same people who were always gathered in places like this. The conversation was the same. Measuring contests, one way or another. In the dangerous neighborhoods of my youth, men had jostled for position with more outward displays of testosterone, but for all the bespoke tailoring and affectations, it was no different here. Learning that had been the key to my first million.

And still all I could think about was Imogen. That ripe mouth of hers that looked like berries and tasted far, far sweeter. And better yet, her scalding softness that had clung to my fingers as she'd clenched and shook and fallen apart.

I had tasted her from my own hand as she sat before me on that table, attempting to recover, and now it was as if I could taste nothing else.

I'd forgotten about Celeste entirely when she appeared before me, smiling knowingly as if we shared a particularly filthy secret. As if we'd last seen each other moments ago, instead of years back.

And as if that last meeting hadn't involved operatic sobs on her part, vicious threats from her father, and a young man's blustery vows of revenge from me.

In retrospect, I was embarrassed for the lot of us.

"How does it feel?" she asked in that husky voice of hers that was so at odds with all her carefully icy blond perfection. But that was her greatest weapon, after all. Hot and cold. Ice and sex. All those deliberate contradictions at once, that was Celeste.

I eyed her entirely too long for it to be polite. "Are you suddenly concerned with my feelings? I somehow doubt it."

Celeste let out that tinkling laugh of hers, as if I had said something amusing. "Don't be silly, Javier."

"I can assure you I have never been 'silly' a single moment in my life. There is little reason to imagine I might start now. Here."

I did not say, *with you*.

"You and I know how this game is played," she told me, managing to sound airy and intimate at once. "There are certain rules, are there not? And they must be followed, no matter what we think of them. I must commend you on thinking to offer for poor, sweet Imogen, the dull little dear. But it will all work beautifully now."

"I have no idea what you're talking about."

"You were wise to wait," she continued gaily, as if the harsh tone I used was encouraging. As if this was an actual conversation instead of a strange performance on her part. "For men with bloodlines as pristine as the count, there can be no stain upon his heirs. Not even a stray whisper. But I have already done my duty and given him spotless children without the faintest bit of scandal attached to their births. Why should he care what I do now?"

I stared at her. So long that the sly, stimulating smile faltered on her lips.

"You cannot imagine that you hold the slightest enticement for me, can you?" I asked with a soft menace I could see very well hit her like a blow. And she was lucky that I knew very well that no matter how disinterested the crowd around us might have seemed, everyone was watching this interaction. Because everyone knew that a decade back, I had made a fool of myself over this woman. "Is your opinion of yourself so high that you honestly believe I would so much as cross a street for you? Much less marry another woman for the dubious pleasure of becoming close to you in some way? I am interested in the Fitzalan name, Celeste. The blood of centuries of kingmakers. Not a single faithless woman I forgot the moment you made your decision ten years ago."

But this was Celeste, who had never faced a moment she couldn't turn into a game—and one in which she had an advantage. Though I was certain I saw a hint of uncertainty in her gaze, it was gone in an instant.

And then I was assaulted with that laughter of hers that had haunted me long after I had left this very house way back when. And not because I had longed to hear it again—ever—but because it was the soundtrack of my own, early humiliation. One of my very few losses.

"You do what you must, Javier," she murmured throatily at me. "Play hard to get if your pride requires it. You and I know the truth, do we not?"

And, perhaps wisely, she did not stick around to hear my answer.

But when they called us into the formal dining hall for the banquet sometime later, I made my way over to Fitzalan and curtly told him that I would not be joining him at the table.

"I beg your pardon," the man said in his stuffy way. I couldn't tell if he looked more affronted or astonished—and this could have been as much because I had approached him without express invitation as what I'd said. "Perhaps you are unaware, Dos Santos, but you are the guest of honor." In case I had failed to pick up on that little dig, that suggestion I didn't know enough to realize the dinner was supposedly for me, he inclined his head in a show of benevolence that made my jaw clench. "You are the one getting married in the morning. It is customary for you to take part."

I forced myself to smile, though it felt raw and unused. "I suspect you will all enjoy yourselves more if you can talk about me rather than to me."

And I only lifted a brow when the other man sputtered in obvious insult.

Not because it wasn't true. But because a man like Dermot Fitzalan was far more offended that anyone might dare call him out on his behavior. Especially if that "anyone" was a commoner like me.

I didn't wait for his response, which no doubt insulted him all the more. I left the crowd without any further awkward discussions, then I made my way through the great house, not sure where my feet were taking me. My thoughts were a strange jumble of Celeste, then and now. The Fitzalan family and how Imogen fit into it, so different was she from her father and sister.

And I even thought about my own family, who it had never occurred to me to invite to take part in this spectacle.

My mother had never taken to the new life I had provided for her. She viewed it all with suspicion and saved the worst of that suspicion for me—especially because of the deal we'd struck. Namely, that I would support her only if she gave up her former life and habits entirely. No opiates. No drink. Nothing but the sweet prison of my money.

"Why must you have a wife such as this?" she had demanded the last time we spoke, when I had subjected myself to my usual monthly visitation to make sure neither she nor my sisters had backslid into habits that would—sooner or later—send the wrong sort of people to my door.

I would pay for their lives as long as they kept them quiet and legal. I would not pay to get them out of the trouble I'd insisted they leave behind in their old ones.

They had all flatly refused to leave Madrid. I had only convinced them to leave the old, terrible neighborhood after a criminal rival had murdered my father—years after I had cut him out of my life because he'd refused to quit selling his poison.

It had taken longer than that for my mother and sisters to kick their own seedy habits. And none of us pretended they'd done it for any but the most mercenary reasons. They all wanted the life I could give them, not the life they'd had—especially not when they might find themselves forced to pay for my father's sins if they stayed there.

But that didn't mean they liked it. Or me.

"The Fitzalan girl is an emblem," I had told my mother, sitting stiffly in the house I kept for her and my sisters. I would not have discussed my marital plans with her at all, but had run out of other topics to discuss with these people who hated me for bettering them. "A trophy, that is all."

"With all your money you can make anything you like into a trophy. What do you care what these people think?"

My mother had a deep distrust of the upper classes. My father had trafficked in too many things to count as the local head of a much wider, much more dangerous operation—and she had always been in peril herself because of it—but she knew that world. On some level she would always trust

the streets more than the fine house I had provided
for her.

Just as she trusted the desperate men who ruled
there more than she ever would me.

"My children will have the blood of aristocrats,"
I had said. "There will be no doors closed to them."

My mother had made a scornful sort of noise.
"No one can see another person's blood, Javier. Unless you spill it. And the only people who worry
about such things are too afraid to do such things
themselves."

My sisters, by contrast, had praised the very idea
of a Fitzalan bride for their only brother, because
they believed that if they pretended to be kind to me,
I might confuse that for true kindness and increase
my generosity.

"It will be like having royalty in the family!" No-
ellia had cried.

"She might as well be a princess!" Mariana had
agreed rapturously.

My sisters had taken to my money with avid, delirious greed. They had not disagreed with me in
years. On any topic. Because they always, always
wanted more. And the longer they lived lavishly at
my expense, the less they wanted to find themselves
tossed back into the dank pit we'd all come from.

Or more precisely: the pit from which I had
clawed my way, with all of them on my back.

I had made the same bargain with all of them. I
would finance their lives as long as their pursuits

never embarrassed me or caused so much as a ripple in the careful life I'd built.

We had always been family in name only. My father had used us all in different ways, either as mules or distractions or accomplices. We were all tainted by the man who had made us and the lies he'd told us.

And worse still, the things we'd done back then, when we'd had no other choices.

Or what I had done to get away from the tragedy of my beginnings.

Of course I hadn't wanted them here, surrounded by so many of Europe's hereditary predators, each and every one of them desperate to find something—anything—they could use to weaken my position in any one of the markets I dominated.

I wandered the Fitzalan house for a long while. Eventually I found myself in the library, cavernous and dimly lit this night. The roof up above was a dome of glass, though rain fell upon it tonight with an insistent beat that made me almost too aware of its potential for collapse. It felt too much like foreboding, so I focused on the books instead. On the shelves that lined the walls two stories high, packed tight with volume after volume I had never read. And had likely never heard of, for that matter.

I was not an educated man. There had been no time to lose myself in books when there were worlds to be won. And yet I felt it tug at me, that insatiable thirst for knowledge that I had always carried in me. Knowledge for knowledge's sake, instead of the kind of intelligence I had learned to assemble to carry into boardrooms and stately homes like this one, so I might best whoever I encountered.

There were times I thought I would have killed for the opportunity to immerse myself in these books men like Dermot Fitzalan had grudgingly read at some or other boarding school in their youth, then promptly forgot, though they always considered themselves far more educated than the likes of me.

Men like him—men like all those who gathered around that dining table even now, no doubt trading snide stories of my barbaric, common ways—preferred to build beautiful monuments to knowledge like this library, then never use them. I didn't have to know a single thing about Dermot Fitzalan's private life to know that he never tarried here, flipping through all these books he had at his disposal simply because he wished to improve his mind. Or escape for an hour. Or for any reason at all.

Meanwhile, I still remembered the first library I had ever entered as a child. We had been rich for our neighborhood because my father ran product, but still poor in every meaningful way. There had never been any cozy nights at home, reading books or learning letters or tending to the mind in any way. Anything I knew I had been forced to pry out of the terrible schools I'd been sent to by law, often without any help from teachers or staff. And any bit of information, knowledge, or fact I'd uncovered in those sad places had been a prize to me.

The library in the primary school I had attended had been a joke. I knew that now. But what I remembered was my sense of awe and wonder when I had walked into a room of books, however paltry the selection or small the room. I hadn't understood that I could read whichever of them I chose at will. It had taken me years to trust that it wasn't another trick like the ones I knew from home. It had taken me a long time to truly believe I could take any book I liked, read it elsewhere, and return it for another without any dire consequences.

Here in this hushed, moneyed place that was palatial in comparison to the libraries in my memory, I pulled a book with a golden spine out from the shelf closest to me, measured the weight of it in my hand, then put it back.

I drifted over to one of the tables in the middle of the floor, set up with seating areas and tables for closer study. The table nearest to me was polished wood, gleaming even in the dim light, and empty save for three uneven stacks of books. I looked closer. One was a pile of novels. Another was of nonfiction, the narrative sort, in several languages. The third, the shortest, was of poetry.

"May I assist you, sir?" came a smooth, deferential voice.

I looked up to find one of the staff standing there, looking apologetic the way they always did. As if they wanted nothing more than to apologize for the grave sin of serving me. I had gotten used to service after all this time, but that didn't make me comfortable with it.

"I am enjoying the library," I said, aware that I sounded as arrogant as any of the men I had left to toast my humble roots in the banquet hall. "Does the family prefer it to remain private?"

"Not at all, sir," the man before me replied, unctuously. He straightened. "The Fitzalan collection is quite important, stretching back as it does to the first recorded history of the family in this area. The most ancient texts are protected, of course, in the glass cases you may observe near the—"

He sounded as if he was delivering a speech from a museum tour. A very long speech. I tapped my finger against the stack of books nearest me. "What are these?"

If the man was startled that I had interrupted him, he gave no sign. He merely inclined his head.

"Those are for Miss Imogen," he said. When I only stared back at him, he cleared his throat and continued. "Those are the books she wishes to take with her into her, ah, new life."

Her new life. With me.

The servant left me shortly thereafter and I told myself that it was time to go back to my rooms. There was business waiting for my attention the way there always was, and I had better things to do than linger in a library.

But I couldn't seem to move. I stared at those

three stacks of books, and it was as if her taste flooded me all over again.

Imogen. Red-gold and wild. Tilting at windmills from all sides.

Because I knew without a shadow of a doubt that had I married Celeste the way I had wanted to do ten years ago, she would not have come to me with a collection of books. Just as I knew that while there was very little possibility that Celeste had spent any time in this library of her own volition growing up, it was a certainty that Imogen had.

There was no reason that should have washed through me like heat.

I picked up the first book of poetry on the stack before me and flipped it open, not surprised that it fell open to a well-worn page. My eye was drawn to a poem that someone—and I was certain I knew who—had clearly liked so much that she'd underlined the things that had struck her most.

"'For here there is no place that does not see you,'" I read, with two lines drawn beneath it in blue ink. "'You must change your life.'"

I closed the book again and left it there, that odd heat still surging in me.

And when I finally started back toward my rooms, I found that I was far more intrigued with this business arrangement of mine than I had been before I'd arrived here.

I had wanted a Fitzalan wife. And I prided myself on getting what I wanted, by any means necessary.

When I had decided at a mere eight years old that I would get out of the stark war zone of my youth, I had done whatever I needed to do to make that happen. I had lied to liars, cheated the cheaters, and had built my own catapult before I rocketed myself straight out of my humble beginnings. It had required a ten-year wait to bend Dermot Fitzalan to my will the way I had done, but I had never wavered.

I had wanted the Fitzalan blood. The Fitzalan consequence and breeding. All the aristocratic splendor that went with a connection to these people and the nobility they hoarded like treasure. I had wanted all of it.

I still did.

But I also wanted Imogen.

CHAPTER FIVE

Imogen

I DIDN'T KNOW how most weddings were meant to go.

I had no idea how they were conducted out there in the world where people made their own choices, but mine was not exactly the festival of emotion and tearful smiles I'd been led to expect by entirely too many bright and gleaming online wedding sites. Or reports from my friends at the convent, whose glittering nuptials had been spread across glossy magazine inserts all over the globe—and as such, had been far too crass and common for my father to permit me to attend.

Not that I had truly imagined it would be otherwise.

I had been presented in my father's rooms first thing, after a long evening and another long morning—already—of what one of my attendants had euphemistically claimed was my opportunity for *pampering*.

If this is pampering, I'd thought a bit darkly as

they'd worked on me as if I was the Christmas goose, *I'm glad this is the first I've had of it.*

But soon enough it had been time to parade me before the only person whose opinion mattered. I had been marched down the hall of the family wing to my father's sitting room and presented. He had been taking his usual breakfast and had deigned to lower the corner of his newspaper, the better to glare at me as he took in my appearance.

He glared at me for a long time.

The attendants he'd ordered to handle the problem that was me had done their duty. I was buffed and shined and beaten to a glow. But the true achievement was my hair. They had straightened it, time and again. They had poured product on it. They had ironed it and brushed it and had blown it out, more than once, so ruthlessly that it still hurt. Then, not to rest on their laurels, they had painstakingly crafted the kind of sweeping, elegant chignon that my sister made look so elegant and easy.

It had taken hours. I felt...welted.

"I see I should have taken you more in hand years ago," my father said acidly, as if my transformation was somehow as upsetting as my usual appearance was to him. "Why have you roamed about in your usual state of disarray all this time if it was possible for you to look like this?"

I didn't think that was a real question. I could still feel yesterday's bruises on my arm, reminding me of the many virtues of silence, but he continued to glare at me until it occurred to me that he meant me to answer it.

"Well, sir, it took hours," I said, awkwardly, given my scalp still ached and the movement of my jaw needed to form words made it worse.

"Yet you felt the reputation and honor of your family did not merit putting in these hours at any other point in your life." My father shifted his glare to the attendant at my side, dismissing me with a curl of his lip. "See to it she does not mess herself up as she is wont to do. I want there to be not so much as a single hair out of place at the ceremony, do you understand?"

"Of course, sir," the attendant murmured, also not looking at me.

Because what I thought about the discussion did not signify. To anyone.

And that, naturally, comprised the entirety of the fatherly advice I received before my wedding.

When I was escorted back to my rooms, they were buzzing with activity. My things were being packed by one set of attendants while another set was responsible for dressing me, and no one required my input on these matters. I let them herd me into the wedding ensemble that had been chosen without my input, muttering to each other as they sewed me into the gown I knew my father had paid a fortune for, as it was nothing short of an advertisement for his power.

But then, Javier had also paid a fortune for this, I

assumed. So I supposed it was best if he, too, got his money's worth in the form of a proper bride. Even I knew that what mattered on occasions like this was perception. No one in this house cared if I was happy. But they likely all cared deeply that I *look* happy. As well as elegant and effortless and *fully a Fitzalan*, the better to honor the blood in my veins.

They might whisper about the ways I was lowering myself. They might titter about *lying down with the dogs*. They would talk among themselves about the variety of ways money was neither class nor nobility and amuse themselves with their feelings of superiority every time they looked at Javier, who could buy and sell them all. A few might even tut sympathetically about the sacrifice I was making.

But if I dared show so much as a hint of trepidation, they would turn on me like the jackals they were.

When I was dressed in acres of sweeping white and draped in fine jewels that proclaimed my father's consequence and taste to all and sundry, my attendants sat me on the bench at the foot of my bed and ordered me not to move. I had been sitting there stiffly, certain I would somehow spill something on myself without actually having anything to spill, when Celeste appeared.

My father felt bridesmaids were gauche—or he was unaware and/or uninterested in the fact I'd actually made friends at school—but I supposed it didn't matter anyway, as Celeste filled all those roles for me.

I sighed a little as she came into the room, careful to maintain my painfully perfect posture, lest I inadvertently wrinkle something. Or make my hair curl. Celeste looked beautiful, as always, and she certainly didn't look as if it had taken hours upon hours and an army to achieve it. She wore a dress in another, warmer shade of white that only enhanced all her blond beauty.

"I'm supposed to be the bride, but I think everyone will be looking at you instead," I said, and smiled at her.

She smiled back. But I couldn't help thinking it took her too long.

"You've made the guests quite curious, you realize," she said, her voice so light and merry I forgot about how long it might have taken her to smile. "How mysterious, to hide away the night before your own wedding. What on earth were you doing? Engaging in some last-minute contemplation and prayer?" She shook her head at me as if I was a silly, hopeless creature she'd happened upon in the gardens and had rescued out of the goodness of her heart. "I hope you weren't continuing the same futile line of thought as yesterday."

"I was enjoying an enforced battery of spa treatments, courtesy of Father." I held up my hand so she could behold the manicure. It wasn't my first manicure, of course, but the women had done more than simply try to shape the ragged nails I had presented them. They had built me new ones, long and elegant enough to rival Celeste's. "I had no idea that so-called pampering could be so painful."

"A wedding is the last day where a girl should look like some kind of dreadful *tomboy*, Imogen," Celeste said with one of her carefree laughs that somehow landed strangely on me. I told myself it was the unnatural way I was sitting there, like some kind of wooden doll. "But don't worry. I can still see the real you in there. A little bit of makeup and pretty nails doesn't change the truth of who you are."

That should have made me smile, surely. But for some reason, instead, it raked over me as if the words had an edge.

An edge I found myself thinking about a little too much as she conferred with my attendants and determined the time had come at last to transport me to my fate. Because once I started thinking of such things, all I could see was that edginess. Celeste looked beautiful, certainly, but she was holding herself as if all her bones had gone brittle in the night.

And when she returned to my side, it again took a moment for her to summon her smile. I didn't let that fact drift away this time, and saw that no matter how she curved her lips, it did not reach her eyes.

A hollow pit seemed to yawn open in my belly.

But I didn't say a word as she motioned for me to rise to my feet and I obeyed. Because I only had one sister. And if she thought as little of me as everyone else in my life, did I really wish to know it? This was the only family I had left.

That hollow pit had teeth, I found. But I endeavored to ignore it.

"Have you seen my groom?" I asked as she linked her arm through mine and led me toward the door, her steps measured and purposeful. "I'm hoping he might have changed his mind."

I was joking, of course. And yet the look Celeste gave me then was…odd. It was as if I'd somehow offended her.

"One thing you should know about Javier, Imogen, is that he never changes his mind," she told me, no hint of her usual laughter in her voice. And no attempt at the light and airy tone I associated so strongly with her. "Never. When he is set upon something, when he has made up his mind, nothing else will do."

That settled uneasily in my gut, right there in that same hollow place, but I didn't question her on it. The brutal way she was holding herself next to me, so rigid and sharp, and the way she looked at me kept me quiet.

And besides, I could still feel the way Javier had touched me. Kissed me. Turned me utterly inside out without it seeming to affect him in the least. While I was still boneless at the very thought—though it was the next day.

I tried to conceal the shaky breath I let out then, but the sharp look Celeste threw my way told me I hadn't fooled her.

She seemed to soften a bit beside me then. Another thing I opted not to prod at. Something else I didn't want to know.

Downstairs on the main floor of the house the great ballroom had been transformed into an elegant wedding venue. My father waited for me at the doors. He swept a critical glance over me when Celeste presented me to him, then slipped inside herself.

"Let's get this over with quickly," he said gruffly, looking down his nose at me. "Before you revert to type."

And without any further conversation, and certainly no inquiries into my state of mind or feelings about this momentous occasion, he nodded to the servants to fling the doors wide. Then he led me down the center of the room.

I had dreamed about this, too. A wedding. *My* wedding. I had spent years imagining how it would feel. What I would do. How magical it would all seem, even if it was an exercise of strictest duty, because it meant the next stage of my life was about to begin.

But *magical* was not the word that came to mind today. I gazed out at the assembled throng of people my father deemed important, all those greedy-eyed men and the haughty women they had brought with them as decoration. The members of my own extended family, those cousins and relations who I wasn't sure I'd recognize out of context, who were entirely too impressed with themselves to do more than stare back at me as if I was inopportuning them by marrying in the first place.

I was tempted to pretend my mother was still alive. And here. And just out of sight, beaming with a magic all her own…

Because there was precious little magic in this room today. And maybe I was the empty-headed, disappointing creature everyone seemed to think I was, because the lack of it surprised me. I suppose I'd imagined that if I was going to dress up like this and play the part of a fairy-tale bride, everyone else might do the same.

But the way the guests all eyed me as if I was nothing more than a piece of meat laid out for their consumption, I thought we might as well have forgone this ceremony altogether, signed a few papers in the presence of an authority somewhere, and been done with it.

I was trying my best not to let any of my thoughts show on my face when my gaze slid—at last—to the center of the makeshift aisle my father had placed between the tables and the man who waited at the head of it.

And it was as if everything else simply…disappeared.

Every time I saw him I was struck anew. This time was worse than before, not least because I felt the impact of him in so many different places. My breasts felt heavy. My stomach was a knot. In between my legs, I was soft and hot at once.

And Javier could tell.

I knew he could.

He watched me approach as if he had already claimed me in every possible manner. As if this was nothing but a formality. Inevitable in every way.

Something about that hummed in me. Like a song.

I forgot about this crowd of mercenaries and snobs, none of whom I would ever have invited to anything had it been up to me. I forgot about the strange way my sister was behaving, all edges and angles when I had expected at least a modicum of sisterly support. I even forgot about my father, who gripped my arm as if he expected me to fling myself out of the nearest window.

None of that mattered. Not while Javier watched me come to him, dressed for him, his gaze like lightning and the storm at once.

As if he had commanded me to do this thing for the simple reason it pleased him.

As if this was nothing more than an act of obedience.

I didn't know why that word somersaulted through me the way it did. Like a sweet little shiver that wore its way down into the depths of me, deep into places I hadn't known were there.

When I had never wanted to obey anyone, and no matter that I'd had no choice in the matter for most of my life. My father. The nuns. The attendants who were less servants than prison wardens. That was the trouble with the way Javier looked at me. That light in his dark eyes made me imagine the kind of obedience that I might choose to give him.

That faint curve to his hard mouth made me wonder what he might give me in return.

We reached the head of the aisle and my father swiftly handed me over to Javier, as if he dared not risk a delay.

My fate, I thought as Javier's hands wrapped around mine. *My doom.*

This monster I had to hope was truly a man, somewhere behind his harsh exterior.

A man who I knew without the slightest shred of doubt would be inside me, and no matter if he was a monster to his core, before I saw another dawn.

I hardly heard a word of the ceremony. The priest intoned this and that. We made our responses.

But nothing was real to me. It was all a kind of dream until Javier slid that heavy gold band onto my finger, as if it was an anchor.

"You may kiss the bride," the priest said severely, as if, were it left to him, he would rid the world of kissing altogether.

But I didn't care about the opinions of a priest I would never see again. Because Javier was pulling me toward him with the same easy confidence my body remembered all too well, bending his head—

And I was filled with a sudden panic.

Did he really want to do this here? What if I responded to him the way I had yesterday? Right here, where everyone could see me... Where my father could watch as I fell apart and shamed him...

I shuddered at the notion. And I saw a corner of Javier's hard, cruel mouth curl as if I'd amused him.

"Be strong, Imogen," he ordered me. "It is only a little while longer until you will leave this house and be entirely in my hands."

"That is not exactly a relaxing thought," I murmured in reply.

That curl deepened, only slightly.

And then he claimed my mouth with a sheer ruthlessness that nearly took my knees out from under me.

He gave no quarter. He made no allowance for the fact we were in public.

Javier, it was instantly clear to me, didn't care who saw me tremble in his arms.

And when he finally raised his head, there was no mistaking it.

He was smiling.

That was what stayed with me as the guests applauded anemically, and the servants swept in to begin serving the wedding breakfast. His ruthlessly male, deeply satisfied smile.

I expected Javier to leave me so he could make his rounds, talking the usual dry business men always did at these things. As far as I knew it was the point of them. But instead, he stayed beside me. So close beside me, in fact, that I could feel the heat of him.

It sank deep beneath my skin, then into my bones,

as if he was that restorative bath I hadn't had last night. Though I did not have to study the man who stood with me—the man I had married, which I couldn't quite take in—to understand that he was nothing so easily comforting as a warm bath.

He was something else altogether.

"Are you very hungry?" Javier asked.

I found the question perhaps more startling than I should have. I chanced a look at him, feeling that same shivery thing wind its way through me, making my knees feel weak. Because his gaze was so direct, so dark and confronting. His nose was a harsh blade, his mouth that hard line, and I felt scraped raw.

And unable to look away.

"No," I managed to say, after taking much too long to stare at him. "I am not hungry at all."

"Then I see no reason to participate in this circus."

I didn't really process what he said, because he wrapped his arm around my back. That heavy arm of his, all roped muscle and lean, leashed power, and I…floated off somewhere. There was nothing but the wild buzz in my head, Javier's arm around me, and that shivery thing that became a flush, working its way over me until I thought that intense heat between my legs was actually visible. Everywhere.

But I came back to reality with a sharp crack when Javier steered me directly toward my father.

"Fitzalan." Javier nodded curtly, which was not the way people normally greeted my father. They tended toward obsequious displays of servility. But that was not Javier. That was not the man I'd married. "You will wish to say your goodbyes to your daughter."

My father drew himself up into the human equivalent of an exclamation point, all hauteur and offense. He gazed at Javier, then turned that same gaze on me.

I flinched. Javier did not.

"I am afraid I am not following you," my father said in the same distant, appalled voice he used when forced to have a conversation with the servants instead of merely issuing demands.

I thought that really, I should have jumped in to assure Javier that my father was not about to launch into any protracted farewells. That had I slipped off without a word he would likely have had no idea I'd gone.

But I couldn't seem to operate my mouth. I couldn't seem to form any words.

And Javier's arm was around me. It was all I could focus on.

I looked away from whatever strange, male showdown was happening between Javier and my father, and found my gaze snagged almost instantly. It was Celeste. She was sitting at one of the tables next to her husband, paying no attention to whatever conversation the count was having with a selection of other European nobles who looked as close to death by heart attack and advanced age as he did. She looked as effortlessly gracious as always, not a single glossy hair out of its place.

It was the look on her face that struck me. It was so...

Bitter, a voice inside me supplied.

And she wasn't looking at the count. Or my father. Or even me.

She was looking at Javier.

I didn't have time to process that, because Javier was moving again, striding away from my father and leaving me no choice but to hurry to keep up or be left behind. Or, more likely, dragged.

"Are we truly leaving our own wedding breakfast?"

I told myself I was breathless from the sudden sprint, that was all.

"We are."

"I didn't think that was allowed."

My breath caught when he stopped, there on the other side of the great doors that led into the ballroom. Because we were suddenly something like alone, out here in the grand foyer that my father always said had offered gracious welcome to a host of Europe's aristocrats. It was a shock after all the eyes that had been on us inside.

And it was even more of a shock because I was suddenly even more aware of how...difficult it was to be near this man.

My palms felt damp. There was that awful, betraying flush that only seemed to sizzle against my skin. There was heat in all the most embarrassing places.

And still I could only seem to manage to stare at the man who had married me as if I was mesmerized. I thought perhaps I was.

"Listen carefully, Imogen," Javier said sternly, but his tone didn't start any alarms ringing in me. There was still all that mad electricity in his gaze. And that hint of a potential curve in one corner of his mouth. "You are my wife now. Do you understand what that means?"

My heart began to pound, hard. "I think I do."

"Clearly you do not."

He reached over and smoothed his hand over the glossy surface of my chignon, grimacing slightly. No doubt because my hair had been shellacked so many times it was now more or less a fiberglass dome.

"This hair," he growled. "What have you done to it? I prefer your curls."

I blinked at that, aware that if he hadn't still been touching me, I would have assumed I was dreaming. No one liked my curls. Not even me.

Especially not me.

"My father wanted me to look the part today," I managed to say despite my confusion. "He has very specific ideas about how a proper Fitzalan heiress is meant to look."

Javier dropped his hand from my head, but it was only to take my hand. The hand where he had slid that heavy ring that I was sure I would never grow accustomed to. He looked at the ring a moment, then he looked from the ring to the place on my arm where my father had grabbed me yesterday. My attendants had done what they could to cover the marks, but he was so close now. I was sure he could see them.

His hard mouth turned grim. And his gaze when it met mine seemed to shudder through me, so intense was it.

"Your new life begins now," he told me in the same dark, gruff way. "You are a Dos Santos wife, not a Fitzalan heiress today. You need no longer concern yourself with the petty concerns of the man who raised you. It does not matter what he likes, what he wants, what he allows."

He toyed with my hand in both of his, almost idly—though I knew somehow that nothing this man did was truly idle.

"This is true of the whole of the world," Javier told me gravely. "It has nothing to do with you. There are no laws, no leaders, no men of power anywhere that you need consider any longer. You are above all of that."

"Above…?" I echoed, as caught up in his intensity as I was in the way he traced my fingers and warmed my hand between his.

"You are mine," Javier told me, that dark gaze like a new vow, hard on mine. "And that, Imogen, is the beginning and end of everything you need to know, from this moment on."

CHAPTER SIX

Javier

I COULDN'T LEAVE that old pile of self-satisfied stone fast enough.

Or its equally smug inhabitants.

We could have stayed for what would likely have been an interminable wedding breakfast, of course. I could have subjected myself to more condescension. I could have stood in that room, choosing not to let myself get offended by every sanctimonious or outright snobbish comment aimed in my direction. I could have pretended I didn't see the way Celeste watched me, as if she still somehow believed that I would waste all these years and all this time chasing after her when she had made her choice.

But I saw no point in playing those games. I already had what I wanted.

I had already won.

A Fitzalan heiress wore my ring as I had told Dermot Fitzalan one would, sooner or later. Nothing else mattered. Nothing in this old house, at any rate.

I had won.

That Dermot Fitzalan had clearly put his hands on what was mine did not surprise me. Men like Dermot wielded their power in every petty way they could. But it was a rage for another time, beating in me like a pulse.

If I gave in to it here, I feared I would raze these stone walls to rubble.

And I didn't know what to do with the notion that the woman at my side—my prize, my wife—was clearly so used to her father's behavior that she not only hadn't commented on it, she didn't look particularly cowed by it, either.

I took Imogen's hand in mine and started toward the grand entrance, ordering the servants to bring my car around as I moved. One thing men like Fitzalan always did well was train their staff to perfection, so it did not surprise me to find my car waiting when we stepped out of the house and, more, another car idling behind it with all of our bags.

I had left instructions, but even if I had not, there was no way all of Imogen's belongings could have fit into a Lamborghini Veneno. Even if they could, the point of a Lamborghini was not the hauling of baggage, as if it was some kind of sedate, suburban SUV.

I handed her into the sports car that was more a work of art than a vehicle, and then climbed into the driver's seat myself, taking pleasure in the way her wedding gown flowed all over the bucket seats and danced in the space between us. It threatened to bury us both in all those layers of finery.

I wouldn't mind if it did.

I liked the dress in the same way I liked the ring I'd put on her finger. I like signs. Portents and emblems. I liked the optics of a Fitzalan girl at my side, dressed in flowing white with my ring—*mine*—heavy on her finger. I could see faces at the windows inside and knew that those same optics weren't lost on our audience.

I had won a major victory and no matter how they looked down on me, these stuffy, inbred aristocrats knew it. In fact, I thought the snobbier they were to my face, the more aware they likely were that my money and its reach had surpassed them in every possible way.

I was a nobody from the gutters of Spain, and yet I was the one the world still bowed to. They were ghosts holding fast to a past few remembered any longer.

But I remembered. And I had done the unforgivable. I had used all my filthy money to buy my way into their hallowed little circles. I had dared to imagine myself their equal.

They would never accept me, but I didn't need acceptance.

I had what I wanted. The past in the form of the lovely aristocrat beside me, and the future we would make together with my influence.

I drove off from the Fitzalan manor house, allowing the car to growl and surge forward like the high-powered, predatory beauty it was. But as I drove it down the lane, half of my attention was on Imogen, who was leaving her childhood home behind her. It would have been normal if she'd shown a bit of trepidation. Or emotion.

Something complicated, even, to match those marks on her upper arm.

But she didn't look back.

I made it to the landing strip where my plane waited for us in record time, exhilarated by all the power and speed I had in my hands again. Especially after these dreary days locked up with ponderous old men who talked about long-gone centuries as if they'd personally lived through them.

It was Imogen I was focused on as we climbed out of the car near the plane, however, not the haunted remains of what had once been Europe's most powerful families.

"You look as if you have seen a ghost," I said as I helped her—and all the filmy layers of her wedding dress—out of the car. I tried to imagine what might upset a sheltered creature like this. "Do you miss your late mother, perhaps?"

She looked a little pale, it was true. Though I couldn't tell if that was an emotional reaction on her part after all, or if it was that damned makeup slapped all over her face, hiding those freckles I liked so much, despite myself.

When I looked closer, however, her copper eyes were sparkling.

"I miss my mother every day," she said. "But that was *fast*."

In that same demure voice she had used at our wedding ceremony. The one that made me almost wonder if the half-wild creature who had turned up in my rooms yesterday had been nothing more than a figment of my clearly oversexed imagination.

I was wondering it again when she smiled at me, big and bright enough to make me very nearly forget all the ways they had muted her for the wedding. "I think I like fast."

I felt that directly in my sex.

"I am glad to hear that. I believe I can promise you fast."

I was not only speaking of cars, but I wasn't sure she took my meaning. She reached over and ran her fingers lightly over the sensually shaped hood of the Lamborghini, then jerked them away. And her smile turned guilty.

"I'm sorry. I shouldn't have touched it."

"You can touch it whenever you like."

"Oh. Are you sure? Only, I was under the impression that most men are very picky about who they let touch."

"They are perhaps choosy about *how* they are touched," I said in a darkly amused voice I made no attempt to hide. "But if you show me a man who claims to be overly picky about where a beautiful woman places her fingers, I will show you a liar."

She curled the fingers in question into a fist, and swallowed hard enough that my gaze drifted to that neck of hers I longed to taste.

When her eyes met mine again, she seemed almost…shy. "Are we still talking about your car?"

I felt my mouth curve. I didn't want to answer that. "If you like."

"I think I may have given you the wrong impression yesterday," she said in a rush, as if it had been difficult for her to get the sentence out. "I don't know why I came to your rooms in the first place. And it certainly wasn't my intention—"

"We will have nothing but time to revisit what happened in my rooms," I told her. "Not a single detail will be overlooked, I assure you."

She looked nervous, and another man might have taken pains to put her at her ease. But I was enough of a bastard to enjoy it.

"Oh. Well. I mean, I think you might have come to a certain conclusion…"

Her voice trailed away as I took her hand again, and I liked that. I liked the way her pulse beat wildly in the crook of her neck, there where I could see it. I liked the heat of her hand in mine and the smoothness of her manicured fingers twined with my hard, calloused ones.

I wanted to be inside her more than I wanted my next breath. I wanted her beneath me, above me. I wanted her in every position I could imagine, and I was a creative man. But they had turned her into a stranger with all that makeup and alien hair.

I didn't like it at all.

"I had intended to jump straight into the sweet satisfaction of consummation," I told her as I led her toward the plane's folded-down stairs.

And I made a split-second decision as we moved. I had planned to take her to my penthouse in Barcelona. It was not the place I considered my true home, but it had seemed to me to be more domestic and private than other properties I had. But she was naive and she was mine. There were marks on her shoulder and they had rendered her unrecognizable. And I wanted things I couldn't quite name.

I followed an urge I hardly understood, and decided I would take her home instead.

"It is not a long flight to the Mediterranean, I grant you." I sounded stiff and strange. I knew it was because I had made a revolutionary decision—when no one was usually granted access to my private island but me. "Still, I thought there would be ample time to take my first taste of wedded bliss."

I could feel her tremble. It was another show of those nerves that lit me up from the inside out, like heat and triumph all at once. Because I liked a little trepidation. I was not an easy man, nor a small one. And Imogen might have indicated that she had already rid herself of her innocence, but I could tell by all these jitters that she had not gotten much experience out of the bargain, no matter who she had been with.

I shoved away the little twist of something darker and stickier than simple irritation that kicked around in me at that thought. Of Imogen spread out beneath another man's body, allowing him inside her...

She was mine. The thought of another's fingers all over her...rankled.

But I was not in the habit of showing my emotions. To anyone. Even myself, if it could be avoided.

"Do you have some objection to the marital bed?" I asked her instead as I allowed her to precede me up the stairs and into the jet. I even attempted to keep my tone...conversational.

I couldn't see her face then. But I saw the way she froze, then started again almost at once, as if she didn't want me to see her reaction any more than I wished to show her mine. I saw how hard she gripped the railing in one hand, and the way she bent her head as she wound as much of the fabric of her heavy dress around her free hand as she could.

I didn't have to see her face to watch the way she trembled. Again. Still.

"I have no objection," she said over her shoulder, in a voice that didn't sound quite like hers. As if her nerves were constricting her throat.

I waited until we had both boarded the plane. I spoke to the captain briefly about the change in flight plans, and when I made my way back into the sleek lounge area, it was to find Imogen seated on one of the leather couches, prim and proper and still awash in all that white.

I threw myself down on the couch facing her, stretching my legs out so that they grazed hers. And then waited to see if she would jerk herself away. Because she was a girl raised to suffer through her duty no matter what, and it had occurred to me that she might very well consider the marital bed one of those duties.

I didn't care to interrogate myself about why, exactly, that idea was so unpalatable to me.

When she didn't move her legs away from mine—when instead she sighed a little bit and stayed where she was—it felt a great deal like another victory.

And the creeping flush that turned her ears faintly pink told me she knew it.

"It looks as if they spent a great deal of time making you into a mannequin today," I said after a long moment spun out into another. "This was certainly not for my benefit. Is this how you prefer to present yourself?"

She took her time raising her gaze to mine, and when our eyes met, hers were cool. I found I missed her wildness. "My father takes his reputation very seriously. You have been saddled with the disappointing Fitzalan daughter, who, I am ashamed to say, requires the aid of a battalion of attendants to look even remotely put together. I assumed you knew."

I didn't think she looked ashamed. If anything,

I would have described her as faintly defiant somewhere behind all that composure.

"Remember what I told you, please. The only disappointment that need concern you now is mine. And I am not disappointed."

I saw her work to keep her face still. Polite and composed, which I knew in her world meant wiped clean of anything but that slight smile. Still, there was emotion in that copper gaze of hers that I couldn't quite read.

"My father does not share your taste, it appears. He insisted that for once in my life I represent the family appropriately." She reached up and patted that smooth helmet of a chignon they'd crafted for her. It didn't move. I doubted a blowtorch could move it. "The main point of contention, as ever, was my hair. It offends my father. He has long been under the impression that I will it to curl for the express purpose of defying him."

I studied her as the plane began to taxi for our takeoff. She looked as elegant as I could have wished. She looked pulled together and carefully curated, the jewel of any collection, even mine. I had no doubt that every man in that ballroom today who had sneeringly referred to her as the lesser of the two Fitzalan sisters had kicked himself for his lack of vision. She looked like what she was: the lovely daughter of an extraordinarily wealthy and powerful man who had been raised to be adorned in gowns and stunning pieces of jewelry. A woman who would function as decoration and an object of envy, whose pedigree was as much in the way she held herself as in the decidedly blue blood that ran in her veins.

She looked perfect, it was true.

But she did not look like Imogen.

She did not look like my Don Quixote bride, who carried windmills in her smile and an irrepressible spirit in her wild red-gold curls.

I wondered how I would have felt about the vision before me now if I hadn't seen the real Imogen yesterday. Would I have been satisfied with this version of my Fitzalan bride? Would I have accepted this smooth version of her, no edges or angles? Would I already be inside her to the hilt, marking my claim upon her tender flesh?

I couldn't answer that. But I did know this: the woman sitting before me looked entirely too much like her sister.

I wanted the Imogen who was nothing at all like Celeste.

And I opted not to look too closely at why that was.

"You say I have not disappointed you," Imogen said as the plane soared into the air, then turned south to cross France, headed toward Majorca and the Balearic Islands off the coast of Spain. "And I appreciate the sentiment. But you're looking at me as if I'm every bit the disappointment my father always told me I was."

"I'm staring at you because you do not look like yourself at all."

"Are you an expert, then?"

"I did meet you before the wedding, Imogen. Perhaps you have already forgotten."

Her ears pinkened yet again, telling me clearly that she hadn't forgotten anything that had happened yesterday. Neither had I.

"I'm not sure why you think that was an example of me looking more myself." She gave the impression of shrugging without doing so. "Perhaps it was yet another costume. The many faces of Imogen Fitzalan."

"Imogen Fitzalan Dos Santos," I corrected her, all silken threat and certainty. I considered her another moment. "Are you planning to maintain *this* costume?"

Her expression was grave. "I shouldn't think so. It took quite a long time. And several battalions of attendants, as I said."

"This I believe."

I stayed where I was, lounging there as the plane hurtled along, my arms stretched out along the back of the sofa. I did not dare move—because if I did, I was quite certain that I would stop caring all that much about what was the real Imogen and what was not. I would put my hands on her and that would be that.

I was not a man given to denying myself much

of anything. So I wasn't entirely sure why I didn't go ahead and do it.

I suspected it had something to do with those marks on her arm and the fact I could not—would not—make myself yet another brutish male she would have to suffer. That was not at all what I wanted from her.

I nodded toward the rear of the jet instead.

"I have no interest in claiming a mannequin," I told her, not certain I recognized my own voice. "Your bags have been taken into one of the state-rooms. I suggest you use this flight to wash away all traces of—" I let my gaze move over her hair, her face "—this."

"'This,'" she repeated. She made a sound that I thought was a laugh, though her expression was clear of any laughter when I raised a brow at her. "Which part of *this*? Do you want me to re-chip my nails? Un-exfoliate my skin?"

"Do something with your hair," I told her, aware that I felt very nearly...savage. It was need and lust mixed up with that possessiveness I didn't quite know how to handle, much less that softer thing I couldn't name. "It doesn't suit you. And I cannot see your freckles."

"That is for your benefit," she replied, quick enough that I felt the lick of it in my sex again, the reappearance of that defiant girl I had met after all. "Surely everyone knows that the sight of a stray freckle on the nose of one's carefully vetted and purchased bride might scar a man for life."

"Wash it all off," I ordered her quietly. "Or I will come back and do the washing myself, and I'm not certain you will enjoy that as much as I know I will."

There was no mistaking the bright sheen of heat in her gaze then, no matter how quickly she dropped it to her lap. For a moment, I thought I could feel flames leap and dance between us, taking up all the oxygen in the cabin.

"That won't be necessary," she said, addressing her lap. Because, no doubt, she imagined that was safer. "I may play the part of a helpless female, Javier, but I assure you I can handle a simple shower."

CHAPTER SEVEN

Javier

I WATCHED HER go in a great cloud of white—moving as quickly as I supposed a person could on an airplane without actually running—and sat where I was for a beat or two after I heard the door to the stateroom open and then shut. Emphatically.

I pulled out my mobile, scrolling through the nine or ten million things that needed my attention immediately, but set it down again without retaining anything. I could feel her, still. Her taste was in me now, and I wanted more.

I wanted so much more.

Even though I had just told her that I wasn't going to help her wash off her bridal costume unless it was necessary, there was a part of me—a huge part of me—that wanted to head back there anyway.

It had never occurred to me that the other Fitzalan daughter would get to me in this way.

I had assumed, in fact, that she would not. Rumors had always suggested that she was awkward and shy, unused to the company of men. I had expected a shy, trembling flower. I had assumed she would require patience and a steady hand and I had been prepared to give her both to get what I wanted.

"The best-bred ones are always crap where it counts," one of the braying jackasses last night had informed the whole of the room as I'd claimed my drink and cautioned myself against swinging on any of the genteel crowd. Not because it wouldn't have been entertaining, but because it would only prove their wildest speculation about my monstrous, animalistic tendencies to be true and I refused to give them such satisfaction. "They make it such a chore. Best to get a few brats on them as quickly as possible and move on to more tempting prospects."

He had not been speaking to me directly. I was not sure he had even been aware I was in the room. The man in question had been a group or two away, perfectly happy to spout such a thing next to the ratchet-faced woman I could only assume was his unhappy wife. The chore herself, in other words.

All the men in the group had laughed. None of the women had.

And I understood this was how things worked in such circles. I understood that the unpleasant submission of wife to husband was a part of what made their world go round, and they all made the best of it. Because there were lands to think of. Inheritances. Bloodlines and legacies.

Easy enough to lie back and think about the comfortable future. Easy enough to suffer a little in order to gain so much in return.

If I understood anything, it was that particular math.

But I was not one of those blue-blooded aristocratic horror shows, a fact they had taken great pains to make sure I understood this weekend. And understand I did. I understood that they would hate me forever because I could take what they wanted, I could claim it as my own, and I could laugh at the notion that it mattered how little they thought of me.

Just as I could dismiss the notion that I needed to treat the aristocratic wife I'd gone to such trouble to buy the way they would have, if she'd been theirs.

I did not need my wife to be my partner, the way I knew some wives were to their husbands, each of them committed to the continuation of their family's influence. And I'd watched my parents sell out each other—and us—too many times to believe in love. But if there was one thing I knew I was good at, and took pride in the practicing, it was sex.

I had been certain that in this, at least, I would manage to work a bit of magic, no matter how repressed and overwhelmed my convent-trained wife appeared.

But that was before Imogen had appeared in my rooms and let me taste exactly how sweet she was. How soft, how hot.

And now I had no doubt at all that whatever else there might be between us, we would always have that deliciously wild heat and everything that came with it.

Windmills all around.

Steady, I ordered myself. There was no point rushing things now when I had waited ten years to get here.

I picked up my mobile again, and forced myself to concentrate on my business. And when I looked up from putting out fires and answering the questions only I could, hours had passed. The plane was landing.

And the woman who walked out of the back of the plane to meet me was the Imogen I remembered. The Imogen I wanted.

Gone was the wedding dress and all its gauzy, bridal splendor. In its place, the first Senora Dos Santos wore another dress like the one she'd had on yesterday when I'd first caught sight of her. Three-quarter sleeves and a hemline no one in their right mind would call provocative. Another pair of glossy, polished leather boots.

But what got my attention most was the hair. Her glorious hair, curling this way and that. I could see that it was still damp, so it looked darker than its usual red-gold, but I hardly minded. Not when I could see the curls I already thought of as mine and, even better, those freckles scattered across her nose.

"Much better," I told her.

"I'm glad you approve," she said, and though her tone was nothing but polite, I found myself searching her face to see if I could locate the edge I was sure I had heard. She looked out the windows. "Where are we?"

"This is the Mediterranean," I said, gesturing out the window at the deep blue surrounding us. "Or more properly the edge of the Balearic Sea, somewhere between Menorca and Sardinia."

She came and sank down on that sofa across from me again. "I've seen pictures of the Mediterranean, of course. But I've never been before."

"I was given the impression you haven't been anywhere."

"My role is to operate as an ornament," Imogen said, without any particular bitterness. "Not to travel the world, collecting experiences. I've had to make do with pictures on the internet."

"I am not at all surprised that your father feared that if you left, you wouldn't return to his tender mercies."

Imogen gazed at me, a faint, sad curve to her lips. "Do you know, I never tried to leave. I'm not sure he was the one who was afraid. He might not have been much in the way of family, but he was the only one I had and I suppose that meant more to me than it should have."

I didn't know why that touched me. I hated that it did. It was one thing to enjoy the fact that we had chemistry, and all the things that could mean for the marriage ahead of us and the sort of sex I had not been looking forward to doing without.

It was another entirely to feel.

Especially when those feelings tempted me to imagine I could relate in any way to a girl who had been raised wrapped up tight in cotton wool and convent walls when I had never been protected or sheltered from anything. On the contrary, my parents had often used me to help sell their poison.

I had learned how to mistrust everything by knowing full well no one could trust me.

"I have an island," I told her coolly, determined that there be no trace of those unwelcome *feelings* in my voice. "It is not very big. But I think it will do nicely enough."

Her gaze moved from the deep blue of the water below to me, then back again, and I could see the trepidation written all over her, stamped into her skin, and yet her anxiety didn't thrill me as much as it had before.

What I could not seem to get straight in my head was why I had presented my island to her in the fashion I had. My own words seemed to hang there in the cabin as the plane lowered toward the ground. Had I truly dismissed it—called it *not very big*? The private Mediterranean island that I had long used as my primary home? It was the one place on the planet I could be sure there would be no eyes on me unless I allowed it. Unless I expressly invited it.

Which I never did.

When I had stood in that house with Imogen's father and all the stuffed shirts he called his contemporaries, there had not been a single part of me that had felt in any way inferior. The very idea was laughable. But let Imogen gaze at me, her freckles uncovered and her curls unleashed because I had demanded she reveal herself to me, and I was undermining myself.

Until this moment, I hadn't known I had such a thing in me.

To say I loathed it was an understatement.

I let that betrayal of myself simmer in me as the plane touched down. I said nothing as we disembarked, allowing Imogen to take her time down the metal stairs, making noises of pleasure as she went.

Because, of course, the island I called La Angelita was—like everything in my collection—a stunning thing of almost incomprehensible, unspoiled beauty. In every direction was the sea, flirting here, beckoning there. The island was barely ten miles across, with the ruins of an old villa of some sort on one end, and high on the cliffs at the other, my own version of a manor house.

Except mine was built to bring the island inside instead of keeping the dour northern French weather out. I had insisted on wide-open spaces, graceful patios, arches beneath red-roof tiles so that everything was airy and expansive. Notably unlike the depressing blocks of flats I'd been forced to call home as a child.

I was proud of this place and the way I'd had it built to my exact specifications. I showed it to very,

very few. My own family had never merited an invitation.

It was possible, I thought as I swung into the Range Rover that had been left for my use by my staff, that I was experiencing a most uncharacteristic attack of nerves myself.

Except Javier Dos Santos, Europe's most feared monster, did not have *nerves*. I did not suffer from any kind of performance anxiety. If I had, I would likely have remained in the neighborhoods of my youth, working a dead-end job if I was lucky. Except young men in those neighborhoods were very rarely *lucky*. They usually ended up dying as my own father had, victims of their own greed and circumstances, slinging poison until it killed them one way or another.

"What a lovely spot," my wholly unaware new wife said, beaming around in all the Mediterranean sunshine as if she hadn't the slightest idea what she was doing to me. I supposed it was possible she didn't, though that suggested she was far more innocent than she had told me she was. "How often do you make it here?"

"La Angelita is my primary residence."

"You mean it's your home."

That was what I called it, but only to myself. The word *home* had too many associations I shied away from. Too many *feelings* attached. "That is what I said."

Her smile only widened at that. It made me… restless.

By the time we drove up to the house itself, sprawled there at the highest point of the island to capture the sweeping views in all directions, I was certain that I had made a terrible mistake. I should have taken her to Barcelona as planned, where I could have been far more certain there was nothing of *me* to be found. I had properties in every major city across the globe, and even more than that in tucked-away, hard-to-reach places. There was a beach in Nicaragua that I had been meaning to visit for some time, for example, to bask in the lack of crowds. There was a mysterious rain forest in Uganda, a spectacular oasis in Dubai.

I should never have brought her *here*.

Especially when I pulled up to the front of the villa and my brand-new wife turned to me, her eyes shining, as if I had given her a gift.

"This is *wonderful*. I thought I would be marched off to some dreary place like my father's house. Somewhere in the pouring rain, very grave and serious and cold, where I would have the opportunity to contemplate the occasion of my marriage in daily sober reflection in the bitter chill. This already seems much better than that."

"Far be it from me to keep you from sober reflection of any kind."

She was still smiling. "I suspect I'll enjoy all

kinds of reflection a great deal more in all this *sunshine*."

"I do not know how you are used to spending your days," I heard myself say as if I was auditioning for the role previously played by her own officious father. "But the first thing you must know about your new life, Imogen, is that I am not a man of leisure. My primary occupation is not finding ways to live like a parasite off the interest of family investments without ever having to lift a finger. I work for my living. I always have and, I promise you, I always will."

I expected her to be offended at that, but instead she gazed at me with a thoughtful expression on her face. "Does that mean I am expected to work, too?"

I scowled at her. "Certainly not."

"That's a pity. I have always wanted to."

"Let me guess." My voice was too harsh. She didn't deserve it. But I noticed that she also didn't seem to react to it, particularly. It was almost as if she was so used to being badly treated that she hardly noticed it at all, and I couldn't say I liked that, either. But I didn't stop. "It has long been your heart's dearest dream to find yourself working in a factory, is it? Backbreaking hours on a factory floor, canning, perhaps? Doing boring, repetitive work, where mindless perfection is required hour after hour after hour? Or let me guess, you would prefer something in a field somewhere? Hideous physical labor among the crops, perhaps. Or there is always the oldest of all professions."

"You are mocking me, of course," she said, in such a calm voice that something I hadn't felt in a decade shifted inside of me, then shot out oily tentacles. *Shame.* I'd last felt it when I'd burned all bridges with my father and used the fire to propel me out of his world, once and for all. "Though now that you mention the oldest profession, you should probably know that the most famous Fitzalan widow of the twelfth century was rumored to have been quite the mistress of her field. I'm sure it was terribly scandalous at the time. Now it's just a story my father likes to tell."

"Even if I wished to put you to work tomorrow, what could you do?" I asked her, still unable to stop myself, and still not sure why I was angry in the first place—and her matter-of-fact talk of ancient prostitutes in her family line only made it worse. "By your own admission you have been trained to be a quiet, genteel decoration, nothing more."

She said nothing for a moment, and I was too aware that we were still sitting in the drive as if frozen there. The sun danced over her, catching those freckles and the gold in her curls. My jaw ached, I was clenching my teeth so hard.

"I am more aware than you could ever be of my own limitations," Imogen told me quietly. With a dignity that felt like a slap. "I know that there is no possibility that I will ever find myself working in a factory. But perhaps I could contribute to the welfare of those who do. There are supposed to be advantages to this much wealth and privilege. Would it be the worst thing in the world if I tried to use them for good?"

I didn't know what I would do if I stayed where I was, caged up in that Range Rover. As if I had somehow shut myself in a box and couldn't find my way out. I slammed out of the vehicle, then stormed around the front of it, my gaze hard on Imogen's.

I opened her door and took her hand as she exited, because she might know her limitations, but I had studied mine. I had determined that of all the things that might trip me up or get in my way in the world I chose to inhabit, manners would not be one of them. I knew which fork to use. How to address whoever might be standing in front of me. How to tie my own damned tie. That was what I had done with the ill-gotten money I'd stolen from my father when I'd left his particular den of iniquity. I'd learned how to look like the man I wished to become.

Then I'd become him.

I was aware that in the places people like Imogen frequented, acts of chivalry were considered the very height of manners. The difference between me and those who practiced it—because the act was what mattered, and the more public the better—was that not one of them had any respect for this woman.

And I was terribly afraid I had more than was wise.

I led my wife into my house, aware of something primitive that beat in me, forcing me to examine it with every step. I had never been possessive like this before. I hardly knew what to make of it.

"I don't suppose you have a library?" she asked me as we crossed the first atrium, where the sun and breeze brought the sea inside. I could hear the hope in her voice.

Just as I could hear how hard she had worked to strip the sound of it from her words.

It pierced me. It was as if she had taken one of the ceremonial blades that hung as decoration on my walls and thrust it straight through me. I thought of those three stacks of books on the table in her father's library. Telling me things about her I wasn't sure I wanted to know.

I didn't understand why it felt like this. As if I could see her, straight through her, and yet was somehow showing her entirely too much of me.

I was not a man who needed to be known. I was more than happy to remain a mystery. I actively courted it, in fact. And at the same time I didn't want to think of Imogen in my house the way she'd been in her father's. Hiding in out-of-the-way places like that library, steering clear of her father's ego and cruelty. And I certainly didn't care for the comparison.

"Yes," I said stiffly. "There is a library. But most of the books in it are in Spanish."

If I expected that to dim her enthusiasm, I was sadly mistaken. If anything, she brightened. "I need to work on my Spanish. I'm not quite fluent yet."

And that was too much. I had an unsolicited vision of Imogen, with her red-gold curls and those sparkling eyes, crawling over me. Naked. And whispering sex words in Spanish. *Mi pequeño molino.*

I didn't think then. My hands did the thinking for me. Before I knew what was happening, they were pulling her to me.

"There is only one word you need to know in Spanish, Imogen." I bent my head. Her lips were a temptation almost beyond imagining. Ripe and sweet, and this time I already knew how good she would taste. "*Sí.* All you need to learn is *sí.* Yes, my husband. Yes, Javier. *Yes.*"

I could feel her tremble. But it wasn't fear. I could tell that from how pliant she was, there between my hands. But if I had been in any doubt, her copper eyes glowed.

I crushed her mouth to mine, as if in a fever.

I didn't care that we were in the wide-open foyer of my house. My staff was paid handsomely for their discretion. But that was the last thought I gave the matter.

I feasted on her. Her mouth was plump and ripe and *mine*, and I had married her, and the fact I was not yet inside her was like torture.

I could feel the pulse of it in my neck. My gut. And in my sex most of all.

I lifted her up, high against my chest, then pulled her thighs around me so she could lock her ankles in the small of my back. I didn't break the kiss, carrying her with me as I moved, my arms wrapped around her to keep her from falling even as she held on to my neck.

I found the first available surface, an incidental table against the nearest wall, and propped her on the edge of it. I kept her at an angle, moving my hands down to find their way beneath that skirt with an urgency I had no desire to temper.

And still I kissed her, deeper and more wild with every stroke. I could taste the addicting heat in her. I could taste every small cry she made in the back of her throat. I could smell the shampoo and soap she had used in the shower on my plane, and they struck me as impossible aphrodisiacs.

There was no time left. I felt mad with the need to claim her. Now.

It was like a drumbeat pounding in my head, and everywhere else besides.

I hooked my fingers on the scrap of lace I found beneath her dress, and tore it off. She made a noise of surprise against my mouth, but my fingers were in the soft heat between her legs, and I felt her turn molten.

I felt clumsy and something like desperate as I fumbled with my own trousers, shoving them out of the way, and letting the hardest part of me spring free at last.

I shifted, and picked her up again, notching the head of my sex against her heated furrow. I angled my head, taking the kiss deeper, thrilling in her uninhibited response to me and those greedy little noises she couldn't seem to stop making.

I didn't understand why this woman got to me the way she did. I didn't understand the things she had made me feel. But I told myself none of that mattered, because there was this.

I gripped her bottom, positioned her perfectly, and then slammed myself home.

And everything changed.

Imogen cried out. Her body, which had been pliant and soft, stiffened.

And I knew.

She was so tight around me it was something like a dream—and I knew.

I muttered a curse and clamped down on the vicious need stampeding through me, bringing myself under control.

"You are a virgin," I bit out, vaguely surprised that I was even able to speak.

Her eyes were slick with unshed tears. Those fine, ripe lips of hers looked vulnerable. Her hands had somehow ended up in fists against my chest.

But still, she tilted up her chin and met my gaze, her curls tumbling over her shoulder as she moved. Because this was Imogen.

"Of course I'm a virgin," she said, and though her voice was scratchy, there was no mistaking the challenge in it. "I was under the impression that was what you paid for."

CHAPTER EIGHT

Imogen

IT HURT.

Oh, how it hurt.

I had meant to tell him, despite my bravado back at my father's house. But I hadn't. And then he had kissed me, sweeping me into his arms, and everything had been so thrilling, so wild—

I felt betrayed that had turned to this. To pain, though the sharpness was fading. But there was still this impossible...*stretching*.

I could feel him inside me. And that part of him, it seemed, was as mighty and powerful as the rest of him.

"You told me you were not a virgin." Javier's voice was the darkest I had ever heard it. Strained, almost. Gritty and harsh, but that seemed the least of my worries. "You made certain to tell me you had given your innocence to another."

It struck me as more than a little ridiculous that we were having a regular conversation. Like this.

Both of us half-naked and parts of us *connected* in that too real, still heavy and unsettling way. I thought that all things considered, I'd very much like to cry. Though I refused to dissolve in front of him. I refused to prove that I was every bit the too-sheltered convent girl he already thought I was.

"I didn't actually *say* I'd slept with someone else," I pointed out.

We were so *close.* I wanted to shove him away from me even as he continued to hold me in the air, wrapped around his big body. And at the same time I wanted to move even closer to him, though I didn't think that was even possible.

And I had no idea why I couldn't catch my breath. I told myself it was the way he continued to stretch me from the inside out. I didn't know if it was the picturing it that made my throat go dry, or the actual sensation.

Javier's expression was far too intent. His dark eyes glittered. "This seems as good a time as any to tell you that I cannot abide lies. Of any kind. Ever. You would do well to remember that, Imogen."

I wanted to tell him what he could do with his dire warnings, but he was inside me and I was...*wide-open* in ways I could hardly process.

"I wanted you to think I had slept with someone, yes," I corrected myself, and then hissed out a little breath when he moved, there below, where I felt exposed and too soft and split open and shivery.

He didn't move much. He pulled the littlest bit out,

then slid in again, and I shifted in his firm grip, ir-
ritably, to accommodate him.

He still held me up and it was odd to think about
that. That he could be so strong that he could continue to hold me like this, my legs wrapped around
him and all of my weight propped on his hands.

And on that other part of him, I supposed.

When I flushed a bit at that, he moved again. Still,
only that very little bit. He did it once, then again.
And again.

"Why would you tell me something like that?"
Javier did not sound angry, exactly. His voice was
too rich. Too dark. It was as if his voice was lodged
inside me, too. "It was never my intention to hurt
you, Imogen. And now I have. I wonder, does this
fit into the story you have in your head? The bar-
barian commoner who took you like an animal and
hurt you on your own wedding night?"

My breath was doing funny things. And he hadn't
stopped that odd little rocking of his. "I don't have
any stories in my head."

"I told you how I feel about lies. They say I am
a brute, do they not? A monster? Did you want to
make sure there could be no debate about that? Do
you plan to report back that I am actually far worse
than you'd imagined?"

"I don't know what you… I would never… I didn't
mean for this to happen."

But I didn't know if that was true. Had I meant it?
After all, I hadn't told him any different and I was the

only one who knew the truth. If there was someone to blame for my discomfort, I was very much afraid it was me. I might not have had much experience— or any, come to that—but I had only met him yesterday and he'd had his hands between my legs with dizzying speed.

I had known the moment he swept me into his arms today where he was headed, hadn't I? The destination might have been fuzzier in my mind. Gauzier, perhaps. But I'd known where we were going.

Maybe he's right, a terrible voice inside me whispered. *Maybe you* wanted *the pain.*

I couldn't tell if the wave of sensation that washed through me then was heat or shame, frustration or need, and I wasn't sure I cared. I moved against him instead, making my own kind of rocking. And something was different then. Something had eased a little, deep inside me, and so I shifted again.

And that time, the wild sensations that swirled around in me were somehow a part of that feeling that stretched me. A part of it and yet something else, too. Something infinitely hotter.

Something that seemed to reflect in Javier's eyes as well.

He gripped me harder. And then he began to move. Or more to the point, he moved *me*.

He lifted me up, then settled me back down on that insanely hard part of him, and waited. When I only sighed a little, then sneaked my hands back up around his neck again, his eyes gleamed.

"I do not wish to play into your stereotypes," he murmured, lifting me and settling me again. Then again. "There are any number of ways this marriage can and may yet be terrible, *mi esposa*, but it will not be because I am a monster in this way. I will not brutalize you in bed. That is the very last thing I would ever wish to do while inside you."

He lifted me up, and put me down again, and every time he did it there was...*more*. More heat. More sensation.

More greed, stampeding through me like some kind of sudden rain shower. I wanted to dance in the storm. I angled myself closer, heedless and needy and amazed, so I could rub the tips of my breasts against the hard wall of his chest.

I did it once, not sure why I wanted to do such a thing until the mad sensation of it made me shudder. I did it again, and he laughed.

Then he picked up his pace.

And I had meant to say more. I had meant to somehow explain the decision I had made. Why I hadn't told him that I was a virgin and why that didn't count as the kind of lie I shouldn't have cared if I told him or not.

But I couldn't concentrate on anything except that glorious heat inside of me. *Him.* The thickness, the length. The way he seemed to fit me perfectly, over and over and over.

I began to feel that same crisis. I began to pant and shake. And all the while he held me as if he could do it forever, thrusting into me over and over again as if I had no purpose on this earth but this. Him. *Us.*

And when I finally broke, it washed over me like another kind of storm, intense and endless. I sobbed out his name, tipping my head forward to bury my face against his neck.

But Javier wasn't done. He shifted me back against the table, angling me so he could hold me against him with one strong arm and brace himself against the wall with his other hand.

And when he thrust into me then, I understood he had been holding back.

This was deeper. Harder.

So wild I wasn't entirely sure I would survive. So hot and glorious I wasn't sure I wanted to survive.

I had already exploded into too many pieces to count, but something about his ferocity lit that fire in me all over again, tossing me from one great crisis straight into the arms of another.

And this time, when it hit me, I screamed.

I felt him pulse within me as he let out a deep groan I only wished was my name, and then he dropped his head to mine.

I had no idea how long we stayed there like that. Panting. Connected.

And for my part, anyway, completely changed.

But eventually, Javier pushed himself away from me. He reached down to release himself from the clutch of my body, and I didn't understand how I could feel…empty. When I had never known what it was to feel *filled* before.

I watched him, half in embarrassment and half in fascination, as he tucked himself away into his trousers again. Then he tugged me off the table and onto the floor, my dress falling down to cover me as if he'd planned that, too.

He didn't say a word. He studied my face for a moment and I regretted the sunlight that poured in from all the open spaces in this house of his, no doubt showing him things I would have hidden if I only knew how. He slid his hand to the nape of my neck, set me in front of him, and propelled me through the sprawling, open house that way.

I should have objected. I should have told him I didn't require that he march me about as if his hand was a collar.

But I was too busy concentrating on putting one foot in front of the other when I felt as if I was made out of froth and need and might shiver to pieces again at any moment. I was surprised I could walk at all. I felt giddy. Silly.

And that didn't change when Javier brought me into a huge, sprawling set of rooms I understood at a glance were his. And likely also mine, though my brain shied away from that, as I had never shared a room—or a bed—with anyone in my life. I couldn't understand how it worked. I'd seen a thousand images of couples tangled around each other, of course, but I couldn't imagine how *I* would settle like that, with arms heavy over me, or my face pressed against someone's back, or…

It was possible I was panicking.

I forced myself to breathe as Javier led me over to a set of the floor-to-ceiling windows that made up the outside walls of this room. This house. Up close, I saw they were actually sliding doors. Javier nodded toward the series of sparkling blue pools outside, each reflecting the blue of the sky above and the sea beyond, and it seemed some kind of dream to me after such a cold, gray January at my father's house. After all the cold, gray Januaries I'd endured there.

It was a gift. It fell through me like the sunlight itself, warming me from the inside.

"The top one is the hottest," he told me, and there were things in his voice I didn't understand. Dark, tangled things. Intimate things. I shuddered. "Go sit in it and soak."

"I didn't bring a bathing costume," I heard myself whisper.

His hand tightened at the nape of my neck, just the slightest bit. Just enough to assure me he felt every shivery, shuddery thing that worked its way through me. "You will not require one, *querida*."

It didn't occur to me to disobey him. He pulled open the heavy sliding door and I walked through it of my own volition. The breeze was warm, or I was warm, and I breathed it all in, deep. I went over to the side of the first, highest pool, and busied myself unzipping boots that seemed too clunky and severe for all this Mediterranean sunlight. He had done away with my panties, another thing I couldn't quite think about directly without blushing, so I pulled off my dress, unhooked my bra, and then went to the edge of the pool. I could see the steam rising off it in the air that could only be the slightest bit cooler. I didn't question it. I eased my way in, sighing a little as the heat enveloped me.

And only as I sat there did I understand the true beauty of these pools and the careful way they had been arranged. Because as I sat, I couldn't see the other pools I knew were there, laid out on different levels here on this cliff high above the water. I could only see the sea.

I thought I had never seen anything so beautiful in person, with my own eyes. There was the sun up above, the blue sea wherever I looked, and the sweet January air that I suspected might be considered cool to those who lived in this climate year-round. But it felt like some kind of prayer to me.

And when Javier slid into the water next to me, I was tempted to imagine that prayer had been answered. I didn't look at him. I was afraid to look at him, I understood, because he was so big and *male* and I could still feel where he'd been inside of me.

And looking at all his flesh, stretched out in such an unapologetically male fashion beside me, might… change me.

We sat in the hot water overlooking the endless stretch of blue for a forever or two. The water soaked deep into my bones, or so it felt. It made me feel as boneless as he did. Maybe it was the sun, washing over the both of us and making me feel all kinds of things I never had before.

Light. Airy. As if I was made of the sunlight and the deep blue water, infused with all that glorious warmth. As if I were connected to the bright pink flowers that crawled up the stone walls of the villa, or the almond tree blossoms, or even the sweet scent of jasmine that danced on the breeze.

"Your life has been lonely, has it not?" he asked after a long while. "Is that why you pretended you weren't a virgin? To confuse the issue?"

And I should have felt ashamed, I thought—but I was too boneless and warm, suspended in all that sunlight and blue.

"Lonely compared to what?" I turned to look at him, my breath catching. And that place between my legs pulsing with fascination. And hunger. "What of your life? You had no friends or family at your own wedding. Are you lonely?"

He eyed me as if I had grown fangs there before him. "I do not get lonely."

"Well, neither do I."

"You told me you miss your mother every day."

The air went out of me at that, but I managed to smile at him anyway. "Yes, but that is no more than another part of me. A phantom limb. I miss her, but it doesn't make me lonely. It reminds me that I loved her." And that she had loved me the way my father had never managed to, but I didn't say that. "I thought you lost your father, too."

"I did." There was an arrested look on his face then. "But I do not miss *him*, Imogen. If I miss anything, it is the father he never was."

I didn't know how long we merely gazed at each other then. I only knew that somehow, I felt more naked than I had before. When Javier moved again, rising from the pool, I wasn't sure if I felt a sense of loss or relief.

"Come," he said from behind me, and I felt as glutted on sunshine as I did shaky and exposed, but I obeyed him.

It was not until I climbed from the pool that I realized that I was showing myself to him. Fully naked, as I had felt in the water. I stopped at the top of the stairs and froze, though the alarm I surely ought to have felt seemed dulled, somehow, as if the sun had taken that, too.

Or that look in his dark gaze had.

Javier had wrapped a towel around his lean hips and something about the contrast between the bright white of the fabric and his olive skin made a different kind of heat tumble through me. And his dark gaze blazed as it moved over me. I felt the heat of it in the fullness of my breasts, the flare of my hips.

He did not speak as he came toward me, then wrapped me carefully, so carefully, in a towel of my own. His expression was grave, that gaze of his intent.

And he made me shudder. Simply by tucking me into the embrace of that towel, then smoothing a few curls back from my face, with a kind of quiet heat that spiraled through me like reverence. And then again when he ushered me over to a table, saw that I was seated with a courtesy that made me ache, and only then raised a finger to beckon his servants near.

I hadn't known I was hungry until the table was covered, piled high with all sorts of delicacies I knew must be local to the region. Cheeses and olives. Marvelous salads made of wild, bright-colored produce. An aromatic chicken, steeped in spices. Almonds and various dishes. I hardly knew where to look. What to taste first.

The food seemed like a part of the sun, the sea. Javier himself. As if there was not one part of this new world I found myself in that wasn't different from the one I had left behind, down to this meal before me with all its sweet, bright colors and savory combinations instead of my father's routine meals made to cater to his vanity in his trim physique, never to tempt him in any way.

Here, with Javier, everything was a temptation.

Especially Javier himself.

He sat across from me, the acres of his bare chest as lush and inviting as the food between us, all mad temptation and sensory overload.

And this man had bought me. Married me. He had taken me from my father's house, and then he had taken me in every other meaning of the term. He had brought me out of the rain, into the light. And now it seemed I found every part of him as sensual as his hands on my body or his hard, cruel mouth and the wicked things it could do against mine. Or that impossibly hard heat of him, surging deep inside me.

He leaned back in his chair, lounging across from me, and I discovered that watching him eat was almost too much for me to bear. Those big, strong hands that I now knew in an entirely different way. Even his teeth, that I had felt graze the tender flesh of my neck. I felt goose bumps dance up and down my arms, then down my spine, and all he did was tear off a crust of bread and dip it into a saucer of olive oil.

Javier was beautiful. Rugged and demanding. He was harsh and he was beautiful and I knew, now, what it was to have him deep inside me.

And I understood that I would never be the same. That I was changed forever, and even if I didn't know quite what that meant—even if I wasn't sure how it would all play out or what it meant to be married at all, much less to a man so different from my father or my sister's husband—I knew that there was no going back to the girl I'd been on that window seat a mere day before, staring out at the rain and dreaming of a safe, sweet stable boy I had barely met.

Here, now, sharing a table with a man like Javier in all the seductive sunlight, it was clear to me exactly how I'd been fooling myself.

There were girlish dreams, and then there was this. Him.

And even as I shivered inside, the shiver turning into a molten heat there where I was still soft and needy, I was glad I knew the difference.

"Let me know when you have eaten your fill," Javier said almost idly, though there was something about his voice then.

Stirring. Intense. As if he knew full well why I couldn't quite sit still.

"Why? Do you not have enough?"

A flash of his teeth. Another man's smile, though in Javier, all I could see was its menace. As if I had insulted him.

"Do I strike you as a man who goes without, Imogen?"

"I only meant… Well, it is an island."

Javier's mouth kicked up in the corner in that way it did, so rarely. His real smile, I knew. Not that other thing he deployed as a weapon.

And this was wired to that molten heat in me, because all I could feel was the fire of it.

"I want to make sure you have your strength, *querida*," he murmured, which did not help the fire at all. If anything, it made it worse. Because I could see the same bright flame in his gaze. "As we have only just begun."

CHAPTER NINE

Imogen

"TODAY WE FLY to Italy," Javier announced one morning weeks later, without warning. "You may wish to prepare yourself for a touching reunion with your family."

He sat, as he always did, at that table out on the terrace overlooking the pools and the endlessly inviting ocean where he preferred to take his breakfast each day. The morning was bright and clear, and yet as I sat there across from him I felt as if I'd been tossed back into the shadows, cold and gray, I thought I'd left behind in France. I must have made some kind of noise, because Javier set aside one of the many international newspapers he scanned each morning and raised his dark brows at me.

"We will be attending a charity ball in Venice. It is an annual opportunity to fake empathy for the less fortunate, something at which your father excels." He studied me for a moment. "Do you have an objection to charity, Imogen? I seem to recall you mentioning you wished to make it the cornerstone of your existence."

I realized I was gaping at him and forced my mouth shut. It was ridiculous that I was reacting like this. There was no reason at all to feel that he had... broken something, somehow, by announcing that we had to leave this place. Particularly for the sort of event that I knew would thrust us both back into the world I had done such a great job of pretending no longer existed these past weeks.

A world that included my father.

I didn't want to leave. I wanted to stay like this forever. The days had rolled by, sunlight and deep blue, the sea air and the soft, sweet breeze.

It was the first holiday I had ever been on in my life.

And yes, of course, I knew it wasn't truly a holiday. Javier worked each and every day. I would have worked myself, had there been something for me to do, but every time I asked he shook his head and then told me to amuse myself as I pleased. So I swam in the pools. I braved the sea on the afternoons when the temperature edged toward hot. I took long, rambling walks down to the ruins on the far end of the island and back, basking in the sunshine and solitude that felt a great deal like freedom.

And anytime he wasn't working, Javier was with me.

Inside me.

All over me, and me all over him, until I could no longer tell the difference between this day or the next. Between his hand and mine, clenched together on the coverlet as he surged inside of me.

I learned how to kneel down and give him pleasure with my mouth. I learned how to accept his mouth between my legs in return. I learned how to explore every inch of his fascinating body with my hands, my mouth, my teeth. We ate the food that always seemed to be taken directly from the heart of all the brightness and calculated to be as pretty as the sun-drenched island around us, and then we rolled around more.

He called me adventurous. He called me *querida*.

I called him my husband, marveled that I had ever thought him a monster, and every day I wondered how any person could be expected to hold so much sensation inside. I could scarcely imagine how my one, single body could contain all these things I felt. All these joys I dared not name.

I didn't want to leave.

I didn't want to return to that cold, cruel world I had left behind without so much as a backward glance, or anything that reminded me of it. I didn't want to start what I knew would be the endless circuit of balls and events that comprised the bulk of the high-society calendar. I had been raised to make that calendar the center of my life. From events like the Met Ball in New York that made the papers to the aristocratic private house parties all over Europe that were only murmured about later, behind the right hands. I had allowed myself to forget that part of my value was appearing at these things, dressed to communicate my husband's wealth and might.

If it were up to me, these weeks on La Angelita would have been a permanent relocation. I wanted us to stay here forever, wrapped up in each other, as if everything else was the dream.

But somehow, I knew better than to say it.

Because this is not his *dream*, a foreboding sort of voice whispered in me, like a blast of cold air down my spine.

"I have always wanted to see Venice," I managed to say.

I even forced myself to smile. To meet that considering gaze of his.

"You are not so convincing."

"I am drunk on the sea air and all this sun." *And you*, I thought, but knew better than to say. Because in all these halcyon days of sex and sun and nights that never seemed to end, there had been no talk of emotion. No whisper of the things I had been raised to consider the province of other, lesser people. "I will have to sober up, that is all."

"I have business that requires my sobriety. You will have nothing to do but party, which certainly doesn't demand any teetotaling should you oppose it. Though I suppose the party itself is your business."

I felt some of the magical glow that had been growing in me by the day stutter a bit, and I resented it. I rubbed the stuttering spot between my breasts and resented that, too.

"If parties are my business, I'm afraid you're going to be deeply disappointed. There were not many parties in the convent."

"Which is why you were sent to that finishing school to top off your chastity with dreary lessons in how to bow, and when, and to whom. You know this very well." Javier set his newspaper aside entirely then, and regarded me for a moment that dragged on so long I almost forgot there had ever been anything but the stern set to his hard mouth and the way his gaze tore into me. "If there is something you would like to tell me, Imogen, I suggest you do so. I have no patience for this passive-aggressive talking around the issue you seem to enjoy."

"There is no issue. I have nothing to tell you."

"Did you think that you would stay on this island forever? Locked away like a princess in a fairy tale? I know I have a fearsome reputation, but I do not believe I have ever tossed a woman in a tower, no matter the provocation." That curve of his mouth caused its usual answering fire in me, but today it felt like a punishment. "I do not believe I have to resort to such things to get what I want. Do you?"

He did not have to resort to anything to get what he wanted from me. I gave it to him with total, obedient surrender. And happily.

And it hadn't occurred to me until now that he

wasn't as swept away as I was. That this was all…
his design.

I had to swallow hard against the lump in my
throat then.

"This is no fairy tale." It cost me to keep my voice
light. "For one thing, Fitzalans are not princesses.
We have long been adjacent to royal blood, but very
rarely of it. Royals are forever being exiled, revolted
against, decapitated. Fitzalans endure."

I felt as if I'd been slapped awake when I hadn't realized I'd fallen asleep. When I'd no idea how deeply
or long I'd been dreaming. It had been weeks since
I'd spared a thought for my father and all the ways
I was likely to disappoint him. Or since I'd worried
about Celeste and the way my favorite—and only—
sister had looked at me on my wedding day. Or how
she'd looked at Javier as we'd left the manor house.

I didn't welcome the return of these preoccupa-
tions.

Or, for that matter, the fact that it had been weeks
since I had given a single thought to the state of my
hair and its defiance of all accepted fashion dictates.
I clipped it up or I let it curl freely, and that was all
the attention I gave the curls that had so dominated
my previous life. I hadn't thought about how badly
I played the part of a graceful, effortless Fitzalan
heiress. I hadn't thought about how different things
would be now that all the snide society wives could
address me directly instead of merely whispering behind their hands as I walked behind my father in my

slovenly way, with the dresses that never quite fell right and the hair that never obeyed. I hadn't thought at all about the many ways I stood in my more accomplished, more beautiful sister's shadow, not for weeks, and now it was likely I would have to do it all over again.

And this time, where Javier could watch and judge the two of us side by side.

I didn't like thinking about it. My stomach rolled at the very notion. I glared down at my coffee and told myself there was nothing wrong with my blurry eyes. Nothing at all.

"We will be attending one of the most famous charity balls of the season," Javier said, his voice darker than it had been before. Darker and somehow more intense. "I was asked to donate a staggering amount of money, and my reward for this act of charity is that I am forced to attend the ball. We will all put on masks and pretend we do not recognize each other when, of course, we do. It is all very tedious. But this time, I will at least be spared the endless advances of the unmarried. And the unhappily married."

I shifted in my chair, still blinking furiously at my coffee.

I had gotten too much sun on my nose, causing even more freckles. I knew my shoulders were in no better state. The sun had brought out more gold and red in my hair, and more curls besides. I tried to imagine myself swanning about a Venetian ballroom, surrounded by women like Celeste. Elegant, graceful women. Silky smooth, sleek women who never worried about dripping their banquet dinners down the front of their gowns, or tripping over the hems of their dresses as they strode about in their impossibly high heels.

I had been to the convent, yes. And I had spent those years in what was euphemistically called finishing school, too. My friends and I regaled ourselves with memories of the absurdities we'd suffered there almost daily in the group chats that kept us connected, shut off as we were in our very different lives. But all the schooling in the world couldn't make me over into Celeste, no matter how many hours I'd spent walking around with a heavy book on my head to improve my posture.

"You are the very definition of a silk purse made from a sow's ear," my father had snarled at my debutante ball. Right after I'd tripped and nearly upended the punch bowl and the table it had been set upon.

That had been the first and last time I had been let loose in aristocratic society, aside from my wedding.

And now this. Where I would bring shame not only upon my father, which I did so often it hardly signified, but on Javier.

This man who knew how to make me sob with joy and need. Who broke me wide-open with more pleasure than the human body should have been able to bear, and yet he did it again and again, and I not only bore it—I craved it. The man who did not want to hear the words that bubbled up in me, so I moaned them out instead in a meaningless, wordless tune.

The very thought of humiliating him the way I knew I was more than likely to do made me want to curl up into a ball. And sob for a few hours.

"Or perhaps you are only comfortable with this marriage when it is conducted in private," Javier said, snapping my attention back to him. "Out of sight. Off on an island no one can access but me. Hidden away where no one can see how far you have fallen."

I blinked at that. Because he sounded almost… hurt. "I don't… I don't want…"

But something had gone horribly wrong. Javier pushed back from the table, rising to his feet and tossing his linen serviette onto the tabletop. He glared down at me in much the same way he had once stared up at me in my father's house. With commanding, relentless fury that should have burned me alive.

And I felt exactly the same as I had then.

Frozen. Paralyzed. Intrigued despite myself.

And in no way immune from that fire.

"You are happy enough to glut yourself on my body," he growled down at me, an expression I didn't recognize on his harsh face. Again, I was tempted to believe that I'd hurt him. *Him*. "You are insatiable. No matter how much I give you, you want more. When you call out for God, I believe you think I am him. But that does not mean you wish to show the world how much you enjoy your slumming, does it?"

He could not have stunned me more if he had overturned the table into the nearest pool and sent me tumbling after it. I felt myself pale, then flush hot, as if with fever. "That's not what I meant at all. I'm not the one who will be embarrassed, Javier. But I'm almost positive you will be."

His mouth was a flat, thin line, but in his gaze I swore I could see pain. "Yes. I will be humiliated, I am sure, when the world sees that I truly married the woman I intended to. That I procured the last Fitzalan heiress. You will have to try harder, *mi reina*, if you want me to believe the stories you tell to hide your true feelings."

I found myself on my feet across from him, my heart kicking at me. I felt panicked. Something like seasick that everything had twisted around so quickly. That I had possibly wounded him, somehow. "I'm not telling you a story."

He said something in guttural Spanish that I was perfectly happy not to understand. Not completely.

"You must have heard what they call me," I continued, holding myself still so he wouldn't see all the shaking I could feel inside of me. "The disappointing Fitzalan sister. The unfortunate one. It was never a joke."

"Enough." He slashed his hand through the air, still staring at me as if I had betrayed him. "We leave in an hour. I have a phone call to make. I suggest you use the time learning how to control your face and the truths it tells whether you are aware of it or not."

He left me then. He stormed off into the villa, and I knew there'd be no point following him. When he disappeared into the wing he kept aside as his office, he did not emerge for hours, and he did not take kindly to interruptions. I had learned these things the hard way.

But today, everything felt hard. I stood where I was for a long time after he'd gone.

That does not mean you wish to show the world how much you enjoy your slumming, does it? he had demanded.

Slumming was the sort of word my father used. It felt like poison in me, leaving trails of shame and something far sharper everywhere it touched. And it touched every part of me. And, worse, corroded the sweet, hot memories of our high blue, sun-filled weeks here.

My eyes blurred all over again.

It had never crossed my mind that Javier even noticed what people like my father thought of him, much less how they might act when he was around. He hadn't seemed the least bit interested in the guests at our wedding, or the things they might have said about him. He hadn't even bothered to stay for the whole of the wedding breakfast, dismissing them all as insignificant, I'd thought.

Yet he'd thrown out that word, *slumming*, as if

he was far less impervious to these slights than I imagined.

I moved out of the sun, as if that could somehow retroactively remove my freckles, and stood there in the cool shadows of our bedroom. I tried to calm my breathing. That wild beating of my heart. But I was staring at that vast bed and I was...lost.

Javier had been intense these past weeks. More than intense. He was demanding, in bed and out. Focused and ferocious, and it sent a delicious chill down my spine and deep into the softest part of me just thinking about it. He turned me inside out with such regularity that I hardly knew which was which any longer. I'd stopped trying to tell the difference.

And now we had to leave here. I had to parade all these things I felt in front of the whole of the world and, worse by far, my own family.

I squeezed my eyes shut, but that didn't help, because then all there was to do was *feel*. And sometimes I told myself that Javier must feel the things that I did. Sometimes I dreamed that he felt as torn apart, then made new, every time we touched.

I wrenched my eyes open again. In the harsh light of day, when I was out on another walk or tucked up beside the pools with one of the Spanish books I was steadily making my way through, I knew better. I had been the virgin, not him. He was a man of vast experience—as I had seen for myself when I searched for him online.

Javier could have anything he wanted. Anyone

he wanted. *The only thing he ever wanted from you*, a nasty little voice inside me whispered, *was your surname*.

Because all the rest of this, I was forced to admit to myself as I stood there—staring blindly at the master bed where I had learned more things about myself than in all my years at the convent—Javier had already had a thousand times over. With women the whole world agreed were stunning beyond measure.

And one of them had been Celeste.

My knees felt wobbly, or maybe it was that my stomach had twisted so hard it threw me off balance, but I found myself sinking down onto the bench at the end of the bed.

Sometimes I told myself sweet little fantasies that Javier might feel as I did, or might someday, but if I was honest, I'd known that was unlikely. I'd pretended I didn't know it, but I did. Of course I did.

Because the only time I had seen any hint of feelings in him was just now.

Now, when we were finally stepping out into public together. Now, when he would have to parade the lesser Fitzalan sister before the world. Maybe it wasn't surprising that our first outing would be to a costume ball. I'd read entirely too many books that used masks and costumes to terrible advantage. Why should this be any different?

Because this was an arranged marriage, plain and simple.

I had spent these weeks in some kind of a delirium. A daydream. Sex and sun and the gleaming Mediterranean—who wouldn't be susceptible?

But Javier had not been in any such haze. Javier had known exactly what he was doing.

He had married me for my name. My fortune, and not because he needed money, but because he was now a part of the Fitzalan legacy.

He had married a pawn, but I had made the cardinal sin of imagining myself a wife in truth. Somehow, in all these weeks, my actual situation had not been clear to me. This was an arranged marriage, and the arrangement was not in my favor.

Javier had not promised me love. He had not promised me honor. And crucially, I realized as I sat there, feeling like the child I had never thought I was until today, he had never promised me fidelity, either.

If Javier noticed my silence—or any of those feelings I was afraid I wasn't any good at hiding, though I tried my best—he gave no sign.

He spent the flight to Venice on his mobile and seemed as uninterested in the fairy-tale city that appeared below us as we landed as he was in me. I pressed my face to the window, not caring at all if that made me look gauche. Or foolish. Or whatever word I knew my father would have used, if he had been there to see my enduring gracelessness.

But I didn't want to think about my father. Or any

of the things that waited for me tonight. All the ways my foolish heart could break—I thrust them all aside.

We were delivered to a waiting boat and that was when my treacherous heart flipped over itself, as if this was a romantic journey. As if any of this was romantic.

I knew it wasn't. But Venice was.

The haughty, weathered palazzos arranged at the edge of the Grand Canal. The piers with their high sticks and the curved blue boats. The impossible light that danced on the dome of Santa Maria della Salute. Gondoliers on the waterways and pedestrians on the arched bridges.

Venice was like poetry. Arranged all around me, lyrical and giddy at once.

The private water taxi delivered us to a private island in the great lagoon.

"Another private island?" I asked, then wished I hadn't when all I received in return was that darkly arched brow of his and that dark gaze that still looked pained to me.

"I prefer my privacy," Javier replied. Eventually. "Though this is not mine. It is a hotel."

I blinked at the pink stone building that rose before me and the rounded church facade that gleamed ivory beside it. There were gold letters on the stones, spelling out the name of some or other saint. "Why are there no other people?"

Javier angled an arrogant sort of look down at me.

And I understood then. He had bought the place out. Because of course he had.

He was Javier Dos Santos. How had I managed to forget all that meant?

I felt flushed straight through as we walked across the empty courtyard, following the beaming staff up from the water and into the hotel itself. This was not like his villa, so open and modern at once. I was struck by the age of the rooms, and yet how graceful they remained, as if to encourage guests to revel in all their mystery and grandeur. And yet it was far more welcoming than my father's residences, all of which had always erred on the side of too many antiques. Cluttered together, simply because they were pieces of history that broadcast his taste in acquisitions.

Our footsteps were loud on the floors. The staff led us to a sprawling suite that encompassed the whole of the top floor, and I told myself it shouldn't feel like punishment when Javier disappeared into the designated office space. Especially since he didn't glance back.

But I summoned a smile from somewhere, because I wasn't alone.

"You have some time before you need to begin getting ready for your evening, signora," my attendant told me in deferential Italian. "Perhaps you would like some light refreshment?"

My smile hurt. "That would be lovely."

I watched as she left, wondering what I looked like to her, this woman who attended the fabulously wealthy and astronomically celebrated occupants of this suite. She must have seen a thousand marriages like mine. Did it begin here, I wondered? Was she rushing down to the kitchens to snigger about the freckled, mop-headed wife who had somehow found herself with a man like Javier Dos Santos in a hotel he'd emptied of all other guests because he preferred the quiet?

But I was making myself crazy. I knew it.

I moved across the grand salon where my attendant had left me, then out through the shutters to the balcony that ran down the length of our suite. And though the air was bracing, especially after all those weeks on the island, I made my way to the edge and leaned against the railing to watch the winter sun turn the sky a pale pink.

If Venice had been pretty in the light, it was magical at dusk.

I breathed in, then let it out, and I thought I felt a kind of easing deep inside.

The city was otherworldly before me, spread out as it must have been at the feet of all the women who had stood on this balcony before me. So many lives, begun and ended right here. All those tears, all that laughter. Panic and fear. Joy and delight. Down through the ages, life after life just as it would continue on after me, and somewhere in the middle of all of it was me.

What was the point of working myself up into a state?

My problem was I kept imagining that I could make my marriage what I wanted it to be when that had never been in the cards, and I should have known that. I did know that.

The day before my wedding I had dreamed of the sweet blue eyes of a stable boy because that was some kind of escape. The day after my wedding I had been punch-drunk on the things my new husband could do to me, the things he could make my body feel, and I had lost myself in that for far too long.

The truth of the matter was that I was a Fitzalan. And no matter if I was the lesser one, I was still a Fitzalan. The women in my family had been bartered and ransomed, kidnapped and sold and held captive across the centuries.

And if my fierce old grandmother had been any indication, not a one of them had dissolved in the face of those challenges. On the contrary, Fitzalan women made the best of their situations. No matter what.

Fitzalans have a higher purpose, Grand-Mère had always said.

There wasn't much I could do about my curls or my clumsiness, but I could certainly work on my attitude. It was perhaps the only thing that was truly mine. Javier had called the party I was headed to tonight my business, and I had been silly to dismiss that.

He wasn't wrong. I had spent years in finishing school learning all the ways an aristocratic wife could use her role as an accessory to her husband to both of their advantage.

"Your greatest weapon is the fact no one expects you are anything but window dressing," Madame had always told us. "Use it wisely, ladies."

And that was why, when I was dressed in my mask and gown and was led out into the main hall to meet Javier that evening, I was ready.

I'd had them pull my hair back into another chignon, though this one did not pretend to be smooth. My curls were obvious, but I thought if they were piled on top of my head it would look more like a choice and less like the accident of birth they were. My inky-black gown had been made to Javier's exacting specifications, my attendants had assured me, clasped high on one shoulder and cascading down on an angle to caress my feet. The mask itself was gold and onyx, and I couldn't deny the little thrill it gave me to see it on my face when I looked in the mirror.

Better by far, however, was Javier's stillness when he saw me, then the gruff nod he gave me.

It told me the same thing I'd told myself while I'd stood outside in the cold and gazed at the fairy tale of Venice laid out before me in the setting sun. Javier might feel nothing for me at all. I needed to accept that. But he wanted me with at least some of the same desperation I felt in me.

It was more than I'd been raised to expect from my marriage. I told myself it would be more than enough.

Because it had to be enough.

"I am ready," I told him. When he held out his arm, I slid my hand through it. And I angled my head so I could look up at him. Then wondered if my breath would always catch like this at the sight of him, even more overwhelming than usual tonight in his dark black coat and tails. "This will be our first society event as a married couple. You must have imagined how it would go."

I could see his dark eyes behind his mask. And that mouth of his, hard and tempting, that I would know anywhere.

"I have."

"Then you must tell me exactly how you see it all in your head, so that I can be certain to do my part."

His gaze was a harsh, glittering thing. He was dressed all in black, including his mask, and yet the way he looked at me made me think I could see all the bright colors of the Mediterranean. "Your part? What is your part, do you imagine?"

"My part is whatever you prefer, of course. You can use me as a kind of weapon to aim however you like. You have no idea how indiscreet men like my father are around people they think are too far below them to matter."

His hard mouth curved slightly, though I did not mistake it for a smile. "I know exactly how they treat people like me, Imogen. And I do not need weapons to handle them. I am the weapon."

"Then it seems we have an arsenal."

When he only watched me in that same stirring and vaguely threatening way, I lifted my chin as if I was preparing myself for a fight. With him.

Even though I knew we were both aware I would never, ever win.

"And if I say all I want from you is decoration?" His voice was silk and menace. It wound around me like the ties he'd used to secure me to that bed of his, one memorable night. "Silence and submission and a pretty smile on your face? What then?"

"You bought me, Javier," I reminded him, and it wasn't until I heard the edge in my own voice that I understood there were all manner of weapons. And that I didn't need his permission to wield them. "I can be whatever you want me to be. I thought that was the point."

CHAPTER TEN

Javier

IF SHE MENTIONED the fact that I'd bought her one more time, it might send me over the edge—and I chose not to question why that was when it was true. I had. And would again. There was no reason at all to resent the way she threw it at me like some kind of challenge.

I didn't like the fact that I was so close to the edge as it was, and we hadn't even made it to the ball yet.

And it didn't help that Imogen looked good enough to eat.

Her hair was more gold than red after our time on La Angelita, even tucked back into a complicated, curling mystery she'd secured to the back of her head with some or other gleaming thing my fingers itched to remove.

She looked like every dream I'd ever had about the wife I would one day win. Or, yes, buy. She was elegant, masked in a way that showed off the aristocratic bones of her face and draped in the finest black that clung to her generous figure in ways that made me ache. She looked gracious beyond measure and far, far out of the league of a drug dealer's son who'd been raised in a gutter. She was as beautiful as she was unreachable, as befit a woman with blood so achingly blue.

Imogen was exactly the wife I wanted on my arm at this or any other society event. She would exude all that Fitzalan superiority without even trying and my dominance would continue unabated and unchallenged from all these men who fancied themselves better than the likes of me.

And she was standing here in front of me talking about what I'd paid for her, as if this union of ours was nothing but the oldest profession in action on a grand scale.

I told myself I was outraged at the insult. When wealthy men hired prostitutes, they were called escorts. And when they bought wives, it was not called a purchase, it was deemed a wise marriage. To think about my choices in any other way suggested I was still in the gutter, despite all my accomplishments.

I assured myself I was furious, but that hardly explained the heaviness in my sex.

The same heaviness that had become my obsession.

The very last thing I wanted to do was take her out of this hotel I'd emptied for my own privacy when it would have been far more entertaining to experiment with that privacy. I wanted to undress her, right here in the cavernous lobby. I wanted to worship every silken inch of her fine, soft body in the filthiest way imaginable. Starting with my mouth.

But there was work to be done. There was always work to be done. Charity balls were only merry social occasions when a man's donations were relatively minor. For me, they were necessary appearances that had to look social and offhanded when they were anything but.

That beguiling, demanding need for her scraped at me with a raw force that was nothing short of alarming, because Imogen was the first woman I'd ever met that I couldn't get enough of—but I ignored it. I had no choice but to ignore it tonight. I kept her arm linked in mine and I led her down to the boat that would take us to the ball, and if my jaw ached from clenching it, that was at least a different sort of ache from the one currently driving me mad.

"I knew it would be beautiful here," she said softly, standing at the rail as the boat cut through the waves, though the night air was cool and whipped at her curls. "But I had no idea it would be *this* beautiful. I had no idea it was possible for anything to be this beautiful."

I moved to stand next to her at the rail, my gaze on the water of the lagoon. And then the canals of Venice before us, inky and dark. Very nearly brooding, this time of year. "I keep forgetting how sheltered your life has been."

"I have been nowhere," she said simply, and I

thought it was the lack of bitterness in those words that cut me the most. "I have seen nothing outside the walls of the convent or that dreary finishing school. Not in person, anyway. And it turns out that you can watch a thousand things on the internet, read as many books as you can get your hands on, and they still won't prepare you for reality."

That word bit at me. *Reality.* Because I knew that on some level, no matter her protestations, she had to be embarrassed that she'd been forced to lower herself to marry a man like me. Of course I knew it. It was one of the defining truths of my life, and it didn't matter that she hadn't said such a thing to me in so many words. I knew it all the same. And I had never felt inferior in her father's house, but it was amazing how easily I slipped into that space when it was only Imogen. When she was the one who looked at me and made me feel that odd sensation I had never felt before—that slippery, uncomfortable notion that I would never get as far away from my wretched origins as I wanted.

It rose between us like a ghost.

And it was a feeling I should have been used to. I was. Still, when it came from Imogen, it made me ache in a new way. I couldn't say I liked it.

Even so, I couldn't keep myself from reaching over to one of the curls that had already escaped. I tucked it behind her ear with a gentleness I knew made me a stranger to myself.

"You mean Venice, of course," I murmured, that

stranger firmly in charge of me now. Was I...*teasing* her? Was I a man who...*teased*? I never had been before. "Or the legendary Mediterranean Sea, perhaps. Not the great many more prurient things a person could read about or watch online, if they wished."

Her gaze met mine, filled with a laughter that I shouldn't have liked so much. I couldn't figure out why I *cared* so much about this woman who came apart in my hands so easily and yet imagined she could fashion herself into some kind of weapon, mine to command.

I didn't want any part of that. The very notion made me have to fight to hold back a shudder.

I told myself it was rage.

Though I knew full well it was connected instead to a hollow place in me that recalled an eight-year-old boy who had understood he would never be as important to those who should have loved and protected him as that poison they took to deliver them into oblivion.

But I refused to think about my parents. Not here. Not now.

There was still so much of the innocent about Imogen as she gazed at me, despite all I had done to claim her for my own. "Of course I mean Venice. What else could I mean?"

"Tell me more about what, precisely, you watched from the confines of the convent. All to better aid your education."

"Documentaries, mostly." Imogen smiled. And it

was worrying, I thought in some distant part of me, how much I liked to see her smile. As if I craved it. As if I was a man who had ever allowed myself to crave anything when I knew full well it was the kind of weakness people like my parents lived to exploit. "About Venice, naturally, in all its splendor. And the Mediterranean Sea, too, now that you mention it."

"They will make a documentary about anything these days," I murmured.

I traced the edge of her mask, the place where the gold and onyx met the soft skin of her cheek. I meant to say something. I was sure I had planned it, even.

But there was something about the water. The echoes and the ancient buildings around us and the particular, peculiar magic of this submerged city, and I couldn't find the words. Or I could, but I didn't want to say them.

I didn't want to name the things that moved in me when I looked at her. Every time I looked at her.

And then we were landing at the palazzo where the ball took place, all gleaming lights and noise spilling out into the winter night, and the moment was lost.

I told myself it wasn't disappointment that crashed over me as I led Imogen toward the entrance of the charity ball and handed off our winter coats. It couldn't be anything like disappointment as I waited for us to be announced, then drew her into the thick of the crowd, because that suggested a depth of emotion I didn't feel.

Because I did not *feel*. I refused.

I had spent all these weeks on the island making certain of this. I had forced myself away from Imogen when I wanted to stay. I had remained in my office for hours though I was distracted and, worse, uninterested.

I kept pretending I could think about something other than getting back inside Imogen, and I kept proving myself wrong.

Tonight appeared to be no exception.

Once inside, I could see the business associates I had come here to meet. Masks did nothing to hide the power that certain men seemed to exude from their very pores no matter what they did to conceal their features. The ball was taking place on the ground-floor ballroom of the ancient palazzo, with mighty old pillars and chandeliers three flights up ablaze with light. There was an orchestra on a raised dais at one end, and enough gold everywhere to make the whole world gleam.

But I wasn't ready. I couldn't quite bring myself to let Imogen loose into this particular pack of wolves. And not because I feared them, but because I was the most fearsome wolf of all and I wasn't nearly done with her. I wished that the weeks we'd spent on my island, happily isolated and removed from all this, had been twice as long.

That felt like another betrayal of the person I had always imagined myself to be, and I wasn't sure I could speak. I was as close to terrified as I'd ever been at what might come out of my mouth if I tried.

Instead, I swept my lovely wife out onto the dance floor. I held her in my arms, gazed down at those perfect lips of hers that I could taste anytime I wished, and told myself my head swam because there were too many people here. It was hot. Noisy.

But she tipped back her head and smiled at me.

And I understood that it wasn't simply that I didn't recognize myself around this woman.

She had made me a liar. A liar with far too many feelings.

Worse, I did nothing with this realization but accept it. And dance.

"I never thought…" Imogen's voice was breathy. Her eyes gleamed brighter than the blaze of lights all around us. "You are a marvelous dancer."

"You sound slightly *too* surprised."

"It's only that I would never have dared imagine you dancing. You're too…"

I felt my brow rise. "Beneath you?"

"Elemental, I was going to say."

What was it about this woman? Why did she turn me into this…sniveling creature who advertised his own weaknesses at the slightest provocation?

"I taught myself," I said. Stiffly, but I said it.

It had been part of those early years, when I'd decided to make a guttersnipe a gentleman. And there was a part of me that expected her to laugh at the notion of a monster practicing a waltz. I might have joined in. But she didn't laugh.

"I took comportment and ballroom dancing lessons. First with the governesses at home, then in the convent. And it was not until I was in finishing school that Madame told us that proper dancing was merely another form of battle."

I studied her face as it was tipped up to mine.

"Battle? I was unaware that finishing school was so…aggressive."

"We find our weapons where we can, Javier."

Her soft voice echoed in my ears long after the song ended, and I was forced to take a step back. To allow her to loop her arm through mine again. To do what I knew I must, rather than what I wanted.

And it occurred to me, with an unpleasant sort of jolt, that I couldn't recall too many instances of doing what I wanted. Rather than what I must.

I had more money than I could ever spend. It would take commitment and effort to rid myself of my wealth. It would take years. Decades.

And yet I still behaved as if I was that kid in the sewers of Madrid. I still expected that at any moment, the authorities might step in and take it all away from me. Denounce me for my father's sins and throw me back where I came from.

I knew better than anyone that we were all of us nothing but self-fulfilling prophecies. And still I allowed those same old obsessions to own me. To shape me. To determine my every move.

I felt far closer to uncertain than I was comfortable with as we drew close to a group containing a man I couldn't help but recognize. He, too, was masked—but his mask was the sort that only drew attention to him, rather than making any attempt at concealing him from view.

"Hello, Father," Imogen said from beside me.

I don't know what I expected. I had seen and loathed those marks this man had left on my wife's skin. I had watched what passed for Fitzalan father/daughter interactions before. Most notably at our wedding, when for all the paternal emotion on display Dermot could have been handing me a large block of granite.

That stoniness was in evidence again tonight.

"It is such a pity that you could not take a little more care with your appearance on a night like this," the old man said, his voice bitter. Cruel. It took me a moment to realize he was speaking to Imogen. "It is your first introduction to society as part of a married couple. Surely you could have done something with your hair."

Imogen only smiled. "I did do something with my hair."

Fitzalan gazed at her with distaste. Then shifted his cold glare to me, as if he expected an apology. Certainly not as if he was giving me one. "I am afraid that no amount of correction has ever worked with this level of defiance. If I were you, I might consider a firmer hand."

Beside me, I felt Imogen stiffen, even though her expression did not change at all. It put me in mind of the sort of weapons she had mentioned. But more than that, Fitzalan dared to speak to me of a *firmer hand*?

I wanted to rip Dermot Fitzalan asunder, here where all the circling wolves could watch. And tear into him themselves when I left him in pieces.

But that was not how men like this fought. Well did I know it. I made a mental note to hit Fitzalan back hard, where he lived.

In his wallet.

And in the meantime, I would force myself to stand here and speak to him as if he did not deserve a taste of his own medicine. My fingers itched to leave their own dark marks on his skin to see how he liked it.

Somehow, though Fitzalan did not deserve it, I kept the true monster in me at bay.

"You are not me," I said coolly to this father who cared so little for his own daughter that he would send her to a marital bed with marks from his own hand. This pompous man who likely had done it on purpose, because it was the next best thing to actually branding Imogen as if she was truly property. "I believe this simple truth fills us both with gratitude, does it not?"

But I didn't hear his response. Imogen excused herself with that same serene smile and her head held high. And instead of attending to the conversation with this man I had cultivated for a decade or more and now had every intention of ruining—instead of taking pleasure in deceiving him or decimating him in turn, one or the other, as long as I came out the winner—I watched her go.

I couldn't seem to stop myself. I couldn't seem to force myself to pay attention to Fitzalan or the men standing with him. I was aware they were talking around me—possibly at me—but I didn't care the way I should have.

The way I always had in the past.

I watched Imogen instead. I watched the light reflect off her glorious curls from those dizzying chandeliers. I watched the easy, unselfconscious way she navigated through the crowd, aware she had no sense of her own grace.

As if I wanted to chase after her like some kind of puppy. Like the kind of soft, malleable creature I had never been.

Like a man besotted, though I knew that was impossible.

And worse, as if what I felt when she walked away from me was grief.

CHAPTER ELEVEN

Imogen

I LOCKED MYSELF in a bathroom stall in the elegant ladies' powder room, perching there on top of the cold porcelain lid and making no attempt to use it.

And then stayed there, where no one could see me.

Or stare at me. Or talk about me where I could hear the unkind note in their voices, yet none of the words, as a group of society women I knew I ought to have recognized had done as I'd found my way here.

Or make disparaging remarks about my hair. My dress. Whatever it was they found lacking in me.

It isn't that you're lacking something, a voice inside of me whispered. It reminded me of the low, husky way Javier spoke to me in the middle of the night when we were wrapped tight around each other in bed, fitted together like puzzle pieces in a way I hadn't been able to visualize before our wedding. And now craved the way I did everything else that involved touching him. *It's that you have the mis-*

fortune of being related to your sister while not ac-
tually being her.

That had the ring of an unpleasant truth. And part
of me wanted to stay where I was for the rest of the
night, the pride and ferocity of the Fitzalan women
be damned, because I was tired of all the compari-
sons. Especially when I was always coming out on
the wrong side of them.

I wanted to stay hidden here, but I knew I couldn't.
I had to gather myself together. I had to smile sweetly,
serenely, while people compared me to my perfect
sister. I had to pretend I was oblivious to the way
people looked at me and the things they said to me
or about me.

But I couldn't seem to make myself move.

That was when I heard the doors open, letting in
a burst of sound of the ball outside. And more than
that, a merry, tinkling laugh that I had known my
whole life.

Celeste.

I surged to my feet, reaching over to throw back
the lock and launch myself out of the stall and at my
sister. She would know what to do. She always knew
what to do. She had somehow gotten that gene while
I had gotten…madly curling, obstinately red hair.

But I froze there, my hand on the lock.

Because I could hear what she was saying and I
suddenly wished I was anywhere in the world but
here.

"Did you see her lumbering furiously across the

floor?" Celeste was asking her companions, all of whom tittered in response. "Storming off with that look on her face in the middle of the ballroom. As if she was planning to break out in some kind of brawl at any moment!"

I had no reason to be standing there, I told myself sternly. No reason at all not to reveal myself. But I still didn't move.

"Your sister does seem a bit *overwhelmed* by things, doesn't she?" asked another woman, in a syrupy sweet voice that I knew I could identify. If I wanted to identify it.

I didn't.

"Imogen is my half sister, thank you very much," Celeste said with a sniff. "I don't know what my father was thinking, messing about with that common trollop."

"I was under the impression Imogen's mother was a duchess or something," someone else murmured, managing to sound apologetic, as if they weren't sure about correcting Celeste even when they were right.

I squeezed my eyes shut. I could feel my hands curled into fists, but I didn't know who or what I wanted to hit. Or even how to hit. My stomach was a terrible knot and there was something too heavy to be simple pain at my temples. I might have thought I was sick, but I knew it wasn't as simple as that.

"Oh, she was the daughter of someone. The Viscount Something, I think. Who can keep track of all those endless British titles?"

That was Celeste speaking. Celeste, who I had always loved. Celeste, who I had trusted.

Celeste, who very clearly hated me.

There was something about that terrible notion that spurred me into action at last.

I shoved open the door and stood there, aware that my chest was heaving as if I'd been running. There was a wall of mirrors in front of me, which allowed me to see exactly how pale I'd become.

It also allowed me to lock gazes with my sister.

Half sister, I reminded myself bitterly.

If Celeste was surprised to see me, she didn't show it. She was dressed like a column of gold tonight, a color that drew attention to her sheer perfection. Her blond hair was elegantly styled in a sweeping updo that I only dared to dream about. She was tall and long and lean. She was the sort of woman who belonged on the covers of a thousand magazines, smiling mysteriously.

Though she didn't smile at me.

"Lurking about in bathrooms now?" she asked, and I couldn't tell if she had always looked at me that way. Or if, after those bright weeks with Javier, I could see all kinds of things in the shadows that I had never seen before.

It was amazing what a difference it made to be wanted.

Loved, something in me whispered, though I didn't dare call it that.

All I knew was that I'd never felt anything like

it before. And that meant that this had always been bubbling in my sister. The way she was looking at me. That awful tone I'd heard in her voice. None of it was new. It couldn't be. And that meant...

"My mother, Lady Hillary to you, was the daughter of a duke," I said quietly, not wanting to accept what all this meant. "As I think you know."

"If you say so," Celeste said dismissively, and then made it worse by rolling her eyes for the benefit of her group of minions.

There was no more pretending. It didn't matter if Celeste had always been like this or if this was something new. She wasn't making any attempt to hide it.

"Are you just going to stand there, Imogen?" Celeste asked after a moment. That was when I realized I still hadn't moved.

"When I first heard you walk in, I thought I might come in for a hug," I said drily. "That seems to be off the table."

Her friends tittered again, but not with her, this time. It was likely childish that I felt that as a victory.

Celeste certainly didn't like it. Her perfect features flushed, and when she turned back to face me, it was as if I had never seen her before. Temper made her face twist.

And for the first time in as long as I could remember, she didn't look beautiful to me at all. I knew what beauty was now. I knew what warmth was. And I couldn't help thinking that I deserved better than spite in a bathroom stall, no matter who it came from.

"Eavesdroppers never hear anything good about themselves, or did you not learn that in all your years locked away in that convent?" Celeste let out one of those laughs. "You certainly didn't seem to learn anything else."

I thought about that look on her face the day of my wedding. I studied the look she wore now. And I remembered what it had been like ten years ago. Her dramatic sobs, loud enough to be heard all over the house, but more important, the fact she hadn't run outside to prevent Javier from leaving. Very much as if it was a performance designed to hasten her own wedding and her own exit from my father's house.

Maybe everything about Celeste was a performance.

But I played my hunch anyway. "Jealousy doesn't become you, Celeste."

This time, that peal of laughter she let out had fangs. I could feel it sink into me and leave marks. Yet I refused to react. Not even when she stepped closer to me, a mottled sort of red sweeping down over her neck to her chest.

"You foolish, absurd child," she said, her voice scathing and pitying at once. "Don't you understand what Javier is doing? He's using you."

I would die before I showed her how that landed on me like one of the walls around us, hard stone crushing me into dust. I stared back at her, lifting my chin, and it occurred to me in some dim part of my mind that I had been preparing for this for years. Hadn't I?

Because my feelings were hurt. There was no getting around that. But I couldn't say I was surprised.

"Yes, Celeste, he is. In much the same way your count used you to fill his coffers and provide him with heirs. Some might call this sort of thing mercenary, but in our family we have always called it marriage."

Something rolled through her. I could see it, ugly and sharp, all over her face.

"You mistake my meaning." Behind Celeste, her group of tittering friends had gone silent. The better to listen so that they might repeat it to the crowd outside, I knew. "The count married me for all the reasons you name, of course. That is simply practical. *Realistic.* But look in the mirror, Imogen. You know what I look like. Do you ever look at yourself?"

"My husband has yet to turn to stone, if that's what you mean."

But my heart beat too hard. Too wild. As if it already knew what she would say.

Celeste leaned closer so there could be no mistake at all.

"Javier could have had anyone's daughter. He is wealthy enough that even royals would have considered him in these progressive times. But he chose you. Have you never asked why?"

I wanted to say something that would hurt her, I realized. But before I could pull myself together enough to imagine what that might be, she kept going.

"He chose the ugly, embarrassing Fitzalan daughter when he is a known connoisseur of only the most beautiful women in Europe."

If she saw the way I sucked in a breath at that, she ignored it. Or worse, liked it.

"Don't you see?" Celeste's voice only grew colder the longer she spoke. Colder. Harder. "He is Javier Dos Santos. He possesses wealth greater than kings. He can do what no other man can, Imogen. He can flaunt an ugly duckling and pretend she is a swan. He can make even the disappointing Fitzalan heiress into a style icon if he so desires. He can do whatever he likes."

I made a sound, but it wasn't a sentence, and in any case, Celeste ignored me.

"Are you truly as simple as you act?" she demanded, pulling herself up to her full height. She shook her head at me, haughty and something like amazed at my naïveté. "It's a *game*, Imogen. Nothing but a game."

For a moment, I heard nothing else. I was aware that Celeste's friends were whispering among themselves. The water was running in one of the sinks. Someone opened the door and I heard the music again. But the only thing I was truly aware of was the scornful way Celeste had said that last bit.

Nothing but a game.

She smiled then, but this time I could see the pity in her gaze. And worse, what I thought was triumph.

"I am sure you find this cruel," she said with great dignity. "But in time, when you have resigned yourself to the reality of your position, I think you'll realize that I was only trying to be kind."

I knew, beyond any shred of doubt, that she was lying.

Or performing, anyway.

And then it didn't matter, because Celeste had always been better at both than me. She swept around, gathering up her skirts and her friends, and left me there to stew in what she'd told me.

And for some reason, I didn't break down when the door shut behind her. Instead, I thought of what it had been like to step off that plane on Javier's island after a lifetime, it seemed, of gray and gloom. I thought of the light. The blue.

I thought of the heat and fire I had found in Javier's arms. Again and again and again.

I took a deep breath, blew it out, and understood deep into my bones that I would rather steal a few weeks of fantasy with Javier whenever he had a mind to indulge himself than subject myself to all of Celeste's chilly, practical "reality."

I would rather be filled with almost too much sunlight to bear. I would rather have wild curls and freckles all over my shoulders. I would rather earn the contempt with which these people treated me than slink around trying to please them and only find myself in the same place.

And there was something about that that felt like liberation.

Because the glory of never fitting in, I realized in a sudden rush, was that I was never *going* to fit in.

And there was no one left to punish me for it.

No governesses. No nuns. My father had no more power over me. He had sold that right. And Celeste… didn't matter. I knew that Javier was determined and relentless enough to have chosen the Fitzalan daughter he wanted no matter what my father might have said about it. And he'd chosen me.

He could have had anyone, as Celeste had said. And he'd still chosen me.

Because he had, he was the only one who mattered.

I knew it was possible—even likely—that Celeste was right and Javier was playing some game. But I wasn't sure it mattered.

I was in love with him either way.

I didn't know a lot about love. Or anything about it, really. Grand-Mère had always banged on about *higher purposes* and *duty*, but *love* had never been a part of the Fitzalan experience. I had assumed that Celeste and I had loved each other the way sisters did, but it turned out I was wrong about that, too. And it was possible there was a part of me that would mourn the loss of a sister it turned out I never quite had and the family that might as well have been carved from the same stone as my father's manor, but I couldn't process that here. Not now.

Because I was in love with my husband.

I was *in love* with him.

And I knew that of the sins women in society marriages like mine could commit, this was perhaps the worst.

Just as I knew that the man who touched me so softly and held me so closely, who made me cry and sob and shake around him, would not want to hear that I loved him.

That didn't change the fact that I did.

And I might have been afraid of the things he made me feel. They overwhelmed me. They were sticky and dark, too much and too wild to contain. I could hardly believe they were real. Or that he was.

I was afraid that he would tell me it was only sex and I was unnecessarily complicating a simple business transaction. I was afraid that he would banish me, send me off to one of his other properties where he could keep me under lock and key and my feelings couldn't inconvenience him. I was afraid that he would laugh at me.

I was terribly afraid that Javier would never look at me again the way he had this morning, when he'd been deep inside of me and I'd thought I might die. That I had died. That I wanted to die. I was afraid I would never feel any of that again.

But I wasn't afraid of him.

And I had spent a lifetime locking myself up before anyone could come and do it for me. I had tried to minimize myself. Hide myself. Stuff myself in a box and be something I wasn't. No matter how many times I'd sneaked off down the servants' stairs, I'd always come back and tried to be what was expected of me.

I wasn't going to do it anymore.

I stepped up to the wide counter, ignoring the sinks before me and keeping my eyes on the bank of mirrors. I peeled the mask off my face and tossed it aside.

Then I reached up, tugged the clip from my hair, and threw it on the counter as well.

I shook my head, using my fingers to help pull out all the pins. I tugged and I pulled, and I tore down the hairstyle I'd considered a compromise. There would be no more compromises.

My hair fell around me, red and gold and curling wildly.

And it wasn't fear that moved in me then, I knew. It wasn't reality according to Celeste.

It was that power I hadn't been able to access, cringing in a bathroom stall.

It was that long, tough line of women who had come before me and survived, one after the next.

It was what had happened in those weeks with Javier. On that beautiful island, the place where I had learned that surrender was not weakness. That it could be a glorious strength.

I had fallen in love with my husband, and that changed everything.

Me most of all.

I didn't think it through. I didn't worry or prepare. I wheeled around, ignored the other women in the powder room who looked my way, and pushed my way back out into the ball.

I was tired of hiding.

Finally, I was tired of it.

I kept my head high, moving through the crowd as if I was made of silk. I paid no attention to the commotion I caused. I kept my eyes on my husband, finding him easily in the crush and then heading straight for him.

Javier, who I had considered a monster.

If he was a monster, I thought now, then so was I. If what it meant was that all these people, these circling wolves, considered us too different from them to matter. But I thought the truth of the matter was that this ball was filled with the real monsters, gorgons fashioned from snobbery and toxic self-regard, bitterness and centuries of living only to get richer.

I kept my gaze trained on Javier. The one man here who didn't belong. He was too…real. Even with a mask on, the truth of who he was seemed to fill the whole of the palazzo. As if everyone else—as if Venice itself—was little more than a ghost.

"You changed your hair," he said in that dark, stirring way of his when I made it to his side. It was the kind of voice that made me wish we were naked together, sprawled out in our bed, where none of this mattered. As if he heard that same note in his voice, he stood straighter. "I didn't realize this was the sort of party that called for different costumes."

"Imogen can always be trusted to do the most embarrassing thing possible," my father sneered from beside him.

I hadn't even seen him there. Because I was free of him, I realized. And it felt like an afternoon of La Angelita sunlight, here in the middle of a cold winter's night.

"My wife's hair—and indeed, my wife herself—cannot be embarrassing, Fitzalan," Javier bit out, with the kind of violence that usually never made it into ballrooms such as this. My father stiffened. My husband's dark eyes blazed. "She is *my wife*. That makes her, by definition, perfect in every way."

"Javier." I liked saying his name. I more than liked it. I waited for him to drag that thrillingly vicious glare away from my father. When it landed on me, it was no softer, but I liked that, too. "I love you."

I saw the way he froze. I heard the astonished laughter from my father and the terribly genteel men around him, none of whom would ever use that word. Or allow it to be used in their presence—especially not in public.

But I had decided not to hide. Not from anyone. Not ever again.

"I love you," I said again, so there could be no mistake. "And I've had enough of this nonsense tonight, I think."

I turned around like some kind of queen. I held my head high as I started across the floor.

And only breathed again when Javier walked beside me, taking my arm in his.

I told myself that come what may—and there was a storm in those brooding dark eyes of his that already felt like thunder inside me, a reckoning I wasn't sure I wanted to face—I would never regret falling in love with my husband.

CHAPTER TWELVE

Javier

I FOLLOWED HER.

I had no choice.

Imogen had made a scene when she'd dropped her little bombshell, and if I let her walk away, they would say I had already lost control of my brand-new marriage. They would smugly agree with each other that it was only to be expected. *Blood will out,* they would assure themselves.

But if I truly didn't wish to lie to myself, I didn't much care what they said.

I cared more that the bomb she'd dropped was still going off inside me.

Again and again and again.

I did not allow myself to think about my hand on her arm. I ignored my body's automatic response to her scent. Or her firm, smooth skin beneath my palm that made me want to touch her everywhere.

I did not feel. I could not feel.

And no matter that I had already felt too much

today already, when she had made it so clear she, too, was as ashamed of me as I was.

You do not wish to feel, something in me whispered harshly. It was the truth. And I had built my life on truth, had I not? No matter the cost?

"Javier—" Imogen began when we stepped outside.

The music inside the ballroom played on, bright against the dark. Light from those chandeliers inside the palazzo blazed, dancing over the stones. But the temperature had dropped significantly, on the water and inside me, and our coats seemed little protection against the cold.

And my wife thought better of whatever it was she had been about to say.

I did not speak when I summoned our transportation and climbed on board. Or when I pried the mask from my face and sent it spinning into the water with a flare of temper I couldn't conceal. We floated back down the Grand Canal, but this time I did not marvel at the palazzos that lined our way. I did not congratulate myself on my climb from grimy flats in Spain to famous canals in Italy's most magical city the way I usually did.

Instead, I stood apart from Imogen and cautioned myself.

I needed to remain calm. Contained.

There had always been a monster in me, but it wasn't the one her father and his pack of wolves imagined.

Whatever this was—this need people had to hurl emotions around like currency, though I had thought better of Imogen—I had never understood it. I had always stood apart from it, gladly.

She had told me she loved me and it beat in me like a terrible drum, dark and dangerous, slippery and seductive.

And I wanted no part of it.

We made it all the way across the lagoon, then docked at our hotel, and I still had not uttered a single syllable.

There were lights around the hotel's courtyard, making it look festive though it remained empty of any guests but the two of us, just as I had wanted it. I waved away the waiting hotel staff and accepted the blast of the January wind—slicing into me as it rushed from the water of the lagoon—as a gift. It would keep me focused.

It would remind me who I was.

"Do not ever do that again," I told her harshly when we had both climbed out of the boat. "It is not up to you to determine when we leave a place. Particularly not if I have business."

"You could have stayed if you wished. I didn't ask you to come with me, I merely said I was done."

She was different. Or she was herself, again—the creature I had beheld what seemed like a lifetime ago now in her father's house in France. She did not avert her eyes as I scowled at her. If there was any meekness in her at all, any hints of that uncertain innocence that had driven me mad on the island, it was gone.

Tonight Imogen was electrifying. Her curls cascaded around her shoulders like fire. Her eyes gleamed in the dark, inviting and powerful at once. She reminded me of an ancient goddess who might have risen straight from the sea in a place like this, gold-tipped and mesmerizing.

I wanted nothing more than to worship her. But that was what I had spent these last weeks doing, and what had I gained?

Protestations of *love*, of all things.

I was more likely to believe her a deity than I was to imagine her *in love*.

I started for the hotel and she was right behind me, hurrying as if she had any chance at all of catching me if I didn't allow it.

"Will you chase me all the way up to our rooms?" I asked her from between the teeth I couldn't seem to keep from clenching when I made it to the stately double doors that discreetly opened at our approach.

"Only if you make me chase you. When I was under the impression that the great and glorious Javier Dos Santos has never run from a fight in the whole of his life."

She was a few feet behind me, looking serious and challenging as she closed the last of the distance between us. She didn't look as if she'd exerted herself unduly running across the courtyard, despite the shoes she wore. Not my Don Quixote bride, who was perfectly happy to tilt at any windmill in sight.

Even if the windmill was me.

I strode inside, not sure what I was meant to do with the temper and din roaring inside of me. Not sure I could keep it locked away as I should, and equally sure I didn't want to let any of it out.

I told myself I didn't know what it was, that howling thing knotting loud and grim within me, but I did.

And I didn't want to feel any of this.

I didn't want to feel at all.

Imogen stayed with me as I made my way across the lobby and I cursed myself for having bought out the whole of the hotel, ensuring that this torturous walk took place in strained silence. I could hear Imogen's shoes against the marble floors. I could hear my own.

And I could hear my heart in my chest, as loud as the roaring sea.

We got into the elevator together and stood on opposite sides as if sizing each other up.

I didn't know what she saw, but I wasn't at all pleased to find she looked no less like a goddess in close quarters.

"What happened to you?" I asked her, too many things I didn't wish to address there in my voice.

"I was born a Fitzalan. Then I got married. Not much of interest happened in between."

What did it say about me that I was tempted to laugh at that?

But I already knew what it said. This had gone on too long, this wildfire situation I should have extinguished the first time I'd seen her in her father's heap of stone and history. I should never have brought her to La Angelita and, once I knew how it would burn between us, I should never have allowed us to stay as long as we had.

The responsibility was mine. I accepted it.

So there was no reason at all that I should have let my head tilt to one side as I beheld her there on the other side of the elevator, dressed in that sweep of deep black, the bright red-gold of her hair a striking counterpoint to the wall of gilt and flourish behind her.

"I think you know that I mean tonight. What happened at that ball?"

She didn't smile this time. And somehow that only drew my attention to her mouth and those berry-stained lips I had tasted time and time again. Yet I could never seem to get my fill.

"My sister suggested I face reality." I couldn't read that gleam in her copper gaze. "I declined."

I hadn't spared a thought for Celeste, I realized now. She would have been there, of course. Annual charity balls like this one were exactly the sort of places Celeste liked to shine. But if she had been there tonight, I had missed it entirely. What was a bit of shine when my wife was like the sun?

I was appalled at the train of my own thought.

"Your sister is the last person on earth I would expect to comment on reality," I said, perhaps more witheringly than necessary. "Given that her own is so dire and uninspiring."

The elevator stopped at our floor, opening directly into our paneled foyer. This time it was Imogen who moved first, sweeping through to the grand salon that made up the bulk of the sprawling hotel suite's public rooms and was even more ecstatically decorated than the hotel lobby, all statuary and operatic sconces.

She moved into the center of the room, leaving me to trail her as she had me down below. I stopped short when I realized that was what I was doing, following her about like some kind of…pet.

And when she turned back to face me, she still didn't look the least bit sorry for what she had done.

"You could have married her. You didn't. Why?"

It took me a moment to stop seething at the notion that I could be the pet in any scenario. And another to comprehend her meaning. When I did, I scowled.

"I believe we already covered this subject in some detail the night before our wedding. If the reality Celeste wished to discuss with you had something to do with me, you should already know she is in no way an expert on that subject."

"Javier. Did she love you?"

The way she asked that question suggested she knew something I didn't. And worse, I didn't get the sense that simple jealousy was motivating the question.

I could have handled jealousy, but I didn't know what *this* was.

"Your sister and I hardly knew each other." It was hard to speak when my jaw was clenched so tight and my hands wanted so badly to curl into fists. "And as time goes on I consider that a great blessing. You must know Celeste better than anyone, Imogen. Do you believe her capable of loving anything?"

She didn't tremble. Not exactly—and yet something moved over her lovely face. "No. I don't."

"But you must step away from all this talk of love," I cautioned her. Though my voice was little more than a growl. "It has no place in an arrangement like ours. It has no place in the kind of lives we lead."

It had no place this close to *me*, I thought, but did not say.

"I'm sorry you feel that way," my blithely disobedient wife replied, without looking the least bit apologetic as she said it. "But it doesn't change the fact that I'm in love with you, Javier."

That torment inside me knotted harder, deeper, and only grew more grim.

"Love is the opiate of the weak," I threw at her. "A gesture toward oblivion, nothing more. It is only sex dressed up to look pretty."

"You are the most powerful man I have ever met. And yet you let my father send you away ten years ago, which tells me you must have wanted to go.

Then you came back and took the only daughter available. Not even the one you'd come for the first time."

I didn't know where she was going with this. I only knew I didn't like it. "You were a virgin, Imogen. I understand why this is difficult for you. Virgins are so easily confused."

"You didn't even know she was there tonight, did you?"

That took me by surprise. Another unpleasant sensation only she seemed capable of producing in me.

"No." I knew I shouldn't have said it when Imogen smiled as if I'd made some kind of confession. "Why do you continue to talk about your sister?"

"They whisper when they think I can't hear, but I do," my wife said in a soft, quiet way that only a fool would mistake for weakness. And I might have been acting the fool tonight, but I wasn't one. "They think you only married me to get to her. I assume she thinks so, too."

"I don't want her." I didn't mean to say that, either, but it was as if that furious growl came out of me of its own volition. "She got what she wanted and so did I. There are no second chances where I am concerned, Imogen. You are either the best or I am bored."

I didn't understand the way she looked at me then. Almost as if I was causing her pain. But she was still smiling, though it was the kind of smile I could feel like a blow.

"I don't care why you married me," she said after a moment. "I don't care if it was purely mercenary or if it was a means to an end like they all think. It doesn't matter to me. What matters to me is what's happened since."

My heart was beating in that strange way again, that insistent and terrible drum. I recognized it. It reminded me of when I was a child, hiding from my parents' demons in filthy hovels, surrounded by too many desperate people.

I shook the memory off. But the fury in me only grew.

"Once again, Imogen, you are confusing sex and passion for something else. But that something else does not exist. It cannot exist."

Her eyes gleamed and I didn't want to understand what I saw there. It made me perilously close to unsteady.

"I love you, Javier," Imogen said. She kept saying it. "I don't think it's something you can order away."

"You might think you do," I gritted out, my voice like gravel. All of me like gravel, come to that. I felt as if I was turning to stone the longer I stood here. "But I know that you do not."

"Don't I?"

"It is a lie, damn you. Love is a weakness. It is a fairy story people tell themselves to excuse the worst excesses of their behavior. Our marriage is based on something far better than *love*."

"Money?" Imogen supplied, and I found that defiance of hers grating tonight. "The fickle support of selfish old men?"

"Neither one of us walked into this marriage with any unrealistic expectations. That is more than any fool who imagines himself in love can say."

"But I want more than easily met expectations," Imogen argued, that gleam in her gaze intensifying. "I want everything, Javier. What's the point otherwise?"

I knew that there were counterarguments I could make. Or better still, I could walk away and end this conversation altogether. I didn't understand why I did neither of those things. Or why I only stood there as if I was rooted to the hotel floor, staring at this wife of mine as if I didn't know her at all.

When I would have said I knew everything there was to know about her. From the poems she read to the sounds she made in the back of her throat when the pleasure I gave her was too much to bear.

"I told you I cannot abide lies," I said, as if from a great distance. "Love *is* lies, Imogen. And I will never build my life on lies again."

She made a noise that could as easily have been a sob as a sigh. She swayed slightly on her feet, and I had to order myself to stay where I was.

My protection was earned, I thought gravely, not given out like candy or sold like street heroin. But it was better when I saw she wasn't toppling over where she stood, felled by the force of her inconvenient emotions. She was squaring her shoulders the way fighters did.

"Show me the lie," she said.

At first I didn't understand what she meant. But as I watched, she reached up and undid the clasp at her shoulder that held her dress on her body. And then, I could only stare in a mixture of astonishment and pure, mad lust as that beautifully inky dress slid down her lush body like a caress and pooled at her feet.

I stood as if I was merely another statue in this salon full of lesser Renaissance offerings. Imogen's copper eyes glowed with more than a mere invitation. I saw in their depths a knowledge I refused to accept.

"I was raised by criminals," I heard myself say as if the words were torn from me. "They trafficked in lies and poison, down in the dirt and the gutters. And love was just another drug they sold, a high that wore off before morning."

I watched as she took that in, waiting for the censure. The revulsion. I watched emotion move across her face like a storm, but she didn't recoil as I expected her to. Instead, she gazed at me with a kind of understanding that I wanted to deny with every breath in my body.

"We can play any game you like, Javier," my wildfire wife told me as if she was the one with years and years of experience. As if I had been the virgin on our wedding day, locked away in a stone house for most of my life, and therefore needed her patience now. "We can start with an easy one, shall we? When I lie, I will stop."

"Imogen."

It was an order, but she didn't heed it.

And I didn't know if I would survive this. I didn't know if I could. I wasn't sure what was worse—if she obeyed me, put her clothes back on, and stopped confusing me with the sight of all that glorious flesh...

Or if she didn't.

As I watched, she unwrapped the particular feminine hardware that held her plump breasts aloft. She reached down and hooked her fingers into the lace that spanned her hips. And I nearly swallowed my tongue as she rolled her panties down the long, shapely legs that I loved to drape over my shoulders as I drove into her. I watched as she kicked the panties aside. And then, still holding my gaze, she kicked off her shoes.

And then my wife stood there before me like the goddess I must have known she was from the very first moment I laid eyes on her on that balcony.

All of those red-gold curls tumbled over her, calling attention to the jut of her nipples and, farther down, that sweet thatch between her thighs in the same bright color.

"Is this a lie?" she asked, all challenge and defiance as she started toward me.

My mouth was too dry. My pulse was a living thing, storming through me and pooling in my sex.

She crossed the floor and stood before me. I could smell the soap she used in her bath and, beneath that, the warmth of her skin. And further still, the sweet, delirious perfume of her arousal.

I could feel my hands at my sides, fisting and then releasing. Over and over. But I didn't reach for her.

"Or perhaps this is a lie," she murmured, her voice hoarse and almost too hot to bear.

But then she put her hands on me, and taught me new ways to burn.

Especially when she ran her fingers over my abdomen, then down farther still, so she could feel the proof of my desire herself.

"What do you want?" I demanded.

I sounded like a man condemned.

"You," she replied, much too easily. "I only want you, Javier. I love—"

But I'd finally had enough.

I heard the noise that came out of me then, like some kind of roar. It came from such a deep place inside of me that I didn't know how to name it.

I didn't try.

I pulled her into my arms, crushing my mouth to hers.

There was no finesse. If I was an animal—if I was the monster they'd always said I was—this was where I proved it. I lifted her from the floor, hauling her into my arms. Then I carried her over to the nearest antique chaise and laid her out upon it. My own sacrifice, once an innocent and now my tormentor.

I followed her down, too far gone to concentrate on anything but my own greed and the way she grabbed my coat as if I was taking too long. And the way her hips rose to meet mine long before I had finished wrestling with my trousers.

There was no time. No playing. There was only this.

There was only the slick, deep slide into all her molten heat.

There was only Imogen.

"Is this a lie?" she whispered in my ear as I lost myself in the rhythm. The deep, sweet thrust in, then the ache of the retreat.

I didn't believe in love. I wanted this to be a lie. That was the only world I knew.

But it was hard to remember what I knew with Imogen beneath me, holding me as tightly and as fiercely as I held her. It was hard to remember my own name as she met me, spurring me on, wrapping her legs around my hips and arching against me to take me deeper.

And the first time she exploded, I kept going. On and on, until she was sobbing out my name the way I liked it.

Only when she convulsed around me a second time did I follow.

But it still wasn't enough.

When I could breathe a little again, I rose. I stripped

off what remained of my evening clothes, and swept my still-shuddering wife up into my arms again. I carried her through the sprawling suite, not letting go of her when I reached the bedroom.

I threw her onto the bed and went down with her, and then, finally, I took back control.

Over and over.

I had her in every way I could imagine.

I tasted her, everywhere. I made her sob, then scream.

I took her into the shower and rinsed us both, then started all over again while the steam rose in clouds around us and the hot water spilled over us both.

I took her and I worshipped her. I imprinted myself on her.

And if there was a lie in any of the things we did, I couldn't find it.

There was pink at the windows when Imogen finally slept, smudges beneath her eyes as she sprawled where I'd left her after the last round. I sat on the side of the bed and forced myself to look away from all of that lush sweetness.

It took some doing.

She would not stop talking of love. She'd kept it up all night, charging that same windmill again and again.

Over and over and over.

And I had spent the whole of my adult life telling myself only the truth. Or trying. I could do no less now.

I was a man, not the monster they imagined I was. Or I believed I was. And no windmill, either. And if there was any creature on this earth who could make me believe in things I knew to be lies, it was this one.

And I could not have that.

I could not bear it.

That was how I, who had never run from anything, found myself out in the Venice dawn.

Running like hell from a woman with red-gold curls, an impossibly sweet smile that cut into me every time I saw it, a defiance that I wanted to taste, not crush—and no sense at all of how she had destroyed me.

CHAPTER THIRTEEN

Imogen

FITZALANS ENDURED.

That was what I told myself when I woke up that morning in Venice and found myself alone.

And without him there to insist on those truths he seemed to hate so much, I lied.

I told myself that he had gone out, that was all. Perhaps to conduct some business. Perhaps to exercise the way he liked to do in the early morning back on the island. I made up all kinds of excuses, but I knew. Deep down, I knew.

He was gone.

His staff arrived at noon.

I didn't put up a fuss. I didn't even ask any questions. I let them collect the bags and lead me out of the empty hotel. I didn't look back.

Nor did I ask where I was headed once they bundled me onto a plane. Not Javier's plane, I noted. Or at least not the one I had been on before. I stared out the window as we soared over Italy and I wondered where he was. Where he had gone to.

And when—or if—he might return.

I didn't know if I was relieved or hurt when we landed back at La Angelita. I held my breath as the car pulled up in front of the villa, telling myself a thousand different and desperate stories about how he'd needed to rush back here, that was all. I would walk inside, past that table in the foyer that still made me blush every time I saw it, and he would be here to greet me with that tiny curve in the corner of his hard mouth...

But he wasn't there.

For the first week, I jumped at every noise. Every time I heard a door open. Every time the wind picked up. Every time a window rattled. I jumped and I expected to see him standing there.

But Javier did not return.

It was sometime into the third week that I found myself sitting in his library, surrounded by books that failed to soothe me for the first time in my life. I was rereading one of my favorite novels, but even that didn't help. I felt thick and headachy and on the verge of tears, all at the same time, and it got worse every day.

I told myself it was a broken heart, that was all. But identifying what was wrong with me didn't help. It didn't fix it. It didn't bring my husband back.

I sat in that library, I thought about the grand sweep of history that had led down through the storied history of the Fitzalan family to me. Here. Alone.

I found myself thinking about my sister and the life she led. How much worse would I feel if I had been married, claimed in such an intimate fashion, and then abandoned…by my sister's husband? By the pursed-mouthed count who never smiled or one of the many indistinguishable men of father's acquaintance just like him?

Despite the way the memories of the ball still smarted, I felt the stirrings of something like sympathy for her. Celeste hadn't had much choice in the matter of her marriage, either. What must it be like for her, shackled to the count until he died, with her unhappiness expected on all sides—and held to be wholly unimportant?

The truth was, I was lucky. I loved Javier. More, I couldn't help believing that he loved me, too, though he might not know it.

If marriage was forever, and I knew full well that this one was—that the kinds of marriages people like me had were always permanent, because they were based on all those distressingly practical things Celeste had mentioned and Javier had echoed—then it didn't matter how long Javier stayed away.

I didn't have to hunt him down. I had already said my piece in Venice.

All I had to do was wait.

The days rolled by, as blue and bright as ever. I found that I was less interested in being on holiday, and started to amuse myself in different ways now that there was no one here to tell me any different.

"I do not think that Senor Dos Santos would like you in his office," the worried butler fussed at me when he found me behind my husband's imposing steel desk, helping myself to Javier's computer and telephone.

"Would he not?"

"The senor is deeply concerned with his privacy, Senora. He does not like anyone in this space when he is not at home."

I beamed at the butler. "Then it is a great shame that he is not here to tell me so himself."

I busied myself as I saw fit. I couldn't put myself to work the way others might, it was true. But I could do my part, so that was what I did.

And if Javier had a problem with the way I was spending his money on what I held to be worthy charities, well. That was his problem. If he wanted to make it *my* problem, he would have to come back to this island and face me.

I filled my days with all that glorious Mediterranean sunshine. I walked through the budding olive groves, looking for signs of spring. I sat in the pools outside the bedroom when dark fell so I could gaze up at the stars and do my best to name them. I walked the length of the unspoiled beaches on all sides of the island, letting all that crisp sea air wash over me, into me.

I spoke to the ocean when no one was around to

hear me. And I always felt it answered me in the relentless way the waves beat against the shore.

It told me stories of endurance, deep and blue
and forever.

It was a full month since the ball in Venice when
I woke as I always did. I stretched out in the vast bed
where I lay alone at night and tortured myself with
memories of those lost, beautiful weeks when I'd
first come here. When I'd given Javier my virginity
and my heart and he'd given me light. I blinked at
the sunshine as it poured in through the windows.

And then, instead of rolling to my feet and perhaps going for a morning swim, I was seized with
the sudden certainty that I was about to be sick.

Horribly sick.

I barely made it across the room and into the bathroom in time.

It was only when I had finished casting out my
misery and was sitting there on the tiled floor with
a cold washcloth against my face that it occurred to
me my evening meal of the night before might not
have been to blame.

I wore nothing but one of Javier's shirts that I had
liberated from his closet so I could pretend he still
held me. And I told myself it was close enough to
him actually being here as I sat there on the floor,
my back against the wall, and spread my hands out
over my belly in a kind of half wonder, half awe.

I hadn't cried since that morning in Venice. Not
since I had finally accepted the fact that Javier had

left me, and had taken myself into the shower because I knew that there was no way he would simply abandon me to my own devices. Not after what he'd paid for me. I knew that his staff would turn up, sooner or later. I needed to be dressed and ready.

But first I had stood beneath the hot spray in that Venetian hotel, loved him, and cried.

These tears were different. There was still that same despair a month later, but it didn't quite take hold of me. Because beneath it was searing, irrepressible joy.

I knew that in my world babies were seen as insurance, not people. Heirs and spares and collateral damage. Too many children and the inheritance was diluted. Too few and tragedy could send all that wealth and history spinning off to someone else's unworthy hands.

But here, now, on the bathroom floor in a villa that was the only place I had ever been truly happy, I forgot all that. I pushed it aside.

"I don't care what they say," I whispered, a fierce promise to the new life inside of me. "I will always love you. You will always know it."

And when I was done, I climbed to my feet and washed my face until there was no trace of tears. Then I called for my attendant and told her what I wanted.

Two hours later, I received a delivery from the nearest chemist's, somewhere on the Spanish mainland. Fifteen minutes after that, I confirmed the fact that I was, in fact, having Javier's child. My child.

Our baby.

And when night fell on that very same day, the sun making its idle way toward the horizon while it painted the sky golds and pinks, I heard the same sort of noise I always heard. And as I always did, I looked up from my favorite chair in Javier's library, expecting to hear the wind or see one of the servants hurrying past.

But this time, he was there.

Right there in front of me after all these weeks.

And he looked murderous.

CHAPTER FOURTEEN

Javier

SHE WAS MAGNIFICENT.

The truth of that slammed into me like a hammer, one hit and then the next, and I had to fight to breathe through it.

Imogen sat with her feet folded up beneath her in an armchair and a thick book open in her lap. I had been standing in the doorway to the library for some time before she noticed me, so enthralled was she with her reading.

It was like torture. She worried her lower lip between her thumb and forefinger. Her skin was flushed from the sun and from the walks the staff had told me she took daily.

And because she was carrying my child.

My child.

She lifted her gaze and instantly made me wonder if she'd known I was there all along.

"Hello, Javier," she said, as if I had happened out for an hour or two. "I wasn't expecting you."

"Were you not?"

I didn't wait for her to answer. I hardly knew what moved in me then. Fury, certainly. Something like panic. And that same dark current of need and longing that had chased me all over the planet and had never let me escape.

She had haunted me everywhere.

And it was worse, somehow, now that we were in the same room.

"I gave up expecting you in the first week," she said, and what struck me was the tone she used. So matter-of-fact. Not as if she was trying to slap at me at all. Which, of course, made it sting all the more. "How long will you stay, do you think?"

"I am told you have news to share with me, Imogen. Perhaps you should start with that."

"News?"

She looked flustered. But I didn't quite believe it.

"Surely you cannot have imagined that you could ask my staff for a pregnancy test without my knowing of it." I stepped farther into the room, expecting her to shrink back against her chair. But she only gazed at me, those copper eyes of hers wiser than before. Or perhaps it was only that I noticed it more now. Now that I knew how completely she could take me apart. And had. "There's nothing you have done in this house that I have not been made aware of within the hour."

She lifted her chin to that challenging angle that I had imagined a thousand times. And that I had wanted to touch a thousand more.

"If you have complaints about the way I choose to donate to the charities of my choice, I'm always happy to sit down with you and discuss it."

"Is this how our marriage works? Is this how any marriage works, do you imagine?"

"If it doesn't, that would also require that you sit down with me. Face-to-face. And have an actual conversation." She lifted one shoulder, then let it drop with an ease I didn't believe. Or didn't *want* to believe, because nothing in me was easy. "It is so hard, I find, to conduct a marriage all on one's own."

I found myself circling her chair, much as I had circled this island again and again since I'd left her in Venice. I had flown all over the world, dropping in on my various business concerns wherever I went. But I always returned to Spain. And I always had to fight myself to keep from coming straight back to this island.

To Imogen.

"That depends, I think, on what marriage it is you think we are having." I was filled with that same dark fury I hadn't been able to shake in all these weeks—the fury I had begun to suspect wasn't fury at all, but feelings. "I bought you for a very specific purpose. I never hid my intentions. You are the one who changed the rules. You are the one who made everything—"

"Real?" she supplied.

"You don't know what real is," I hurled at her, and I could hear that I was spinning out of control. That quickly. That completely. But I couldn't stop it. "You have no idea what it is to grow up the way I did."

"No, I don't."

I was so taken aback by her agreement that I froze. Then watched as she rose to her feet, the light, summery dress she wore flowing around her. I was struck by the expanse of her legs and her bare feet with toes tipped pink. I couldn't have looked away from her if my life depended on it.

She had become no less of a goddess in the time I'd been away, and it was worse now. Because I knew she carried my child. I couldn't see it, not yet, but I knew.

It made her more beautiful. It made everything more beautiful, and I didn't know how to handle it. Beauty. Love. Imogen.

This is what I knew: I wasn't built for happiness.

"I don't know the precise details of how you grew up, or every last thing your childhood did to you. I know the bare bones. I know what little you told me when you thought you could use your past as a weapon. And I'm never going to know more than that unless you tell me. Just as there are things you don't know about me that you never will unless you're here to ask. But it doesn't matter, because our marriage will last forever. That's the benefit of a business arrangement." She waved an airy hand that I didn't believe and wanted, badly, to take hold of with my own. Yet I refrained. "We have all the time in the world to tell each other everything, one detail at a time."

Yet it was the phrase *business arrangement* that I couldn't get past, not this light talk of *details* when I had already shared more with her than anyone else in this life I'd scraped together by force of my own will. *Business arrangement* was in no way an incorrect way to describe our marriage, and yet it scraped over me, then deep inside me, as if it was hollowing me out.

"Why am I not surprised that a few weeks of solitude and the threat of motherhood are all it takes?" I shook my head. "No more talk of love."

And it was not until my own, bitter words hung there in the quiet of the library between us that I realized how much I'd been depending on hearing more of those protestations she'd thrown my way in Venice.

Or how certain I'd been that she'd meant all those words of love I'd refused to accept.

Imogen's eyes blazed copper fire. "You have everything you want, Javier. The Fitzalan heiress of your dreams. A child on the way to secure your legacy. And right when I was tempted to get ideas about my station, you put me in my place. Mention the word *love* and that's a quick way to get a month of solitary confinement." She wrinkled up her nose. "I can't complain. I've spent a lot of time in far worse prisons than this."

"La Angelita is hardly a prison."

"I love you, you fool." But she sounded something like despairing. "It isn't going to go away just because you do."

"You didn't come after me."

I heard the harsh, guttural voice. And it took me a long, hard kick from my own heart to realize it was mine.

"Javier..." she whispered, one hand dropping to cradle that belly where my child already grew.

And something in me...broke.

"You have ruined me," I told her, as if I was accusing her of some dark crime. "You took my home. You took my heart when I did not think it existed to be taken. And you left me with nothing. You talk of prison? I have spent these past weeks flying from country to country, looking at every last part of my collection...and none of it matters. None of it is *you*. The whole world is a prison without you in it."

Her lips parted as if she was having trouble believing what she was hearing. "You can have any woman you choose."

"I chose you!" I thundered. "Don't you understand? All I ever wanted was to *collect*. To win. You don't have to feel anything to do these things, you just have to have the money. And I always had the money. That is why, whatever the thing is, I have the best of it. But then you stormed out of a bathroom in Venice ranting about love and nothing has been the same since."

"Because I love you," she said again, in that same *absolutely certain* way she had in Italy.

Those words had chased me around the world. And back to her side again.

"I don't know what that is," I told her, the emotion in my own voice nearly taking me to the floor. "But I do know that a collection is not a life. And I want to live. I want to know my own child. I want to raise him. Not the way my parents raised me, feral and grasping and out of their minds. And not the way your father raised you, shut up behind one set of walls or another. I want to *live*, Imogen. And I think that must be love because I cannot come up with any other name for it."

That had come out like another accusation, but she only whispered my name. And it sounded like a prayer.

Maybe that was why I found myself on my knees before her after all, my hands on that sweet belly of hers that I had tasted and touched, and now held the start of our very own family. The future. All the hopes and dreams I'd told myself I was far too jaded to allow.

"I cannot live with lies," I told her, tipping my head back so I could look up at all those curls. And her shining eyes. Her lips like berries, trembling now. "But I do not know how to feel."

"But you do." She held my face between her hands and made me new, that easily. "You call it sex. You dismiss it. But it isn't just sex, Javier. It never was."

"How would you know this? You have never had anyone but me."

"Because I know."

And again, she struck me as a creature far wiser than her years. Far more powerful than the sheltered girl she had been.

I understood then.

She was all those things and more. She was everything I needed.

I had bought a bride, but she had given me life.

"I think I looked up to that balcony and lost myself," I told her, fierce and sure.

"I married a monster," she whispered in return, her face split wide by that smile of hers that made the floor seem to tilt beneath me, "but it turned out, he was actually the very best of men. And better yet, mine."

"Yours," I agreed. "Forever."

She sank down before me, wrapping her arms around my neck, and something inside me eased.

"Forever," Imogen said solemnly. "And you can leave me alone if you must, Javier. I am quite happy with my own company—"

"I have wandered the world alone and without you for quite long enough. I do not plan to do it again."

"I love you," she whispered.

There was a truth in me then. I had been denying it for a long time. And I couldn't pretend that it didn't unnerve me, but the truth of it haunted me all the same.

It had chased me all over the world. It had never let me go.

Just as she wouldn't, I knew. Marriages like ours were built to last.

And ours was far better than most.

"I love you, too, Imogen," I said in a rush.

But when she smiled, brighter than the Mediterranean sky outside, I said it again.

And found it got easier every time.

"I love you," I said as I fit my mouth to hers in wonder.

"I love you," I told her as I smoothed my hands over the belly where our child grew, and pressed my lips to her navel.

And then I showed her what it was to love her, inch by beautiful inch, all across that beautiful body of hers.

I loved her and I'd missed her and I showed her all the ways that I would never, ever leave her again, right there on the floor of the library.

And when she was shaking and laughing and curled up against me, her face buried in my neck as she tried to catch her breath, I understood at last.

The Dos Santos marriage was a love match, not merely good business, and it would confound them all. It would add to our legend. It would make me more powerful and it would make Imogen an icon, and none of that would matter half so much as this. Us.

The way we touched each other. The children we would raise together. The life that we would live, hand in hand and side by side, forever.

This was love. It had always been love. This passion was our church, these glorious shatterings were our vows.

And we would say them, every day and in every language we knew, for the rest of our lives.

* * * * *

If you enjoyed
My Bought Virgin Wife
by Caitlin Crews,
you're sure to enjoy these other
Conveniently Wed! stories!

Claiming His Wedding Night Consequence
by Abby Green
Bound by a One-Night Vow
by Melanie Milburne
Sicilian's Bride for a Price
by Tara Pammi
The Prince's Wedding Night Heir
by Lucy Monroe

Available now!

#3693 A DEAL FOR THE SICILIAN'S DIAMOND
Conveniently Wed!
by Michelle Smart
Aislin will do anything to secure money for her sick nephew—even pose as billionaire Dante's fiancée at a society wedding. Yet soon their explosive passion rips through the terms of their arrangement, leaving them both hungry for more...

#3694 THE PRINCE'S RUTHLESS WEDDING VOW
by Jane Porter
When Josephine rescues a drowning stranger, she's captivated. Until it's revealed that he's Prince Alexander, heir to the throne of Aargau... Now the threat of scandal means this shy Cinderella must become a royal bride!

#3695 INNOCENT QUEEN BY ROYAL COMMAND
Claimed by a King
by Kelly Hunter
King Augustus is shocked when his country delivers him a courtesan. But Sera's surprising innocence and undisguised yearning for him pushes Augustus's self-control to the limits. Now he won't rest until Sera becomes his queen!

#3696 BILLIONAIRE'S PRISONER IN PARADISE
by Annie West
Finding herself incognito and captive on Alexei's private island, Princess Mina must convince him *she's* his future bride. But after a night in the Greek's bed, there's more at stake than her hidden identity—her heart is at Alexei's mercy, too!

YOU CAN FIND MORE INFORMATION ON UPCOMING HARLEQUIN® TITLES, FREE EXCERPTS AND MORE AT WWW.HARLEQUIN.COM.

HPCNM0119RB

Get 4 FREE REWARDS!

We'll send you 2 FREE Books plus 2 FREE Mystery Gifts.

USA TODAY BESTSELLING AUTHOR
Jennie Lucas
The Baby the Billionaire Demands

USA TODAY BESTSELLING AUTHOR
Carol Marinelli
The Innocent's Shock Pregnancy

Harlequin Presents® books feature a sensational and sophisticated world of international romance where sinfully tempting heroes ignite passion.

FREE
Value Over
$20

YES! Please send me 2 FREE Harlequin Presents® novels and my 2 FREE gifts (gifts are worth about $10 retail). After receiving them, if I don't wish to receive any more books, I can return the shipping statement marked "cancel." If I don't cancel, I will receive 6 brand-new novels every month and be billed just $4.55 each for the regular-print edition or $5.55 each for the larger-print edition in the U.S., or $5.49 each for the regular-print edition or $5.99 each for the larger-print edition in Canada. That's a savings of at least 11% off the cover price! It's quite a bargain! Shipping and handling is just 50¢ per book in the U.S. and 75¢ per book in Canada.* I understand that accepting the 2 free books and gifts places me under no obligation to buy anything. I can always return a shipment and cancel at any time. The free books and gifts are mine to keep no matter what I decide.

Choose one: ☐ **Harlequin Presents®**   ☐ **Harlequin Presents®**
                  Regular-Print   Larger-Print
                  (106/306 HDN GMYX)   (176/376 HDN GMYX)

Name (please print)

Address   Apt. #

City   State/Province   Zip/Postal Code

Mail to the **Reader Service:**
IN U.S.A.: P.O. Box 1341, Buffalo, NY 14240-8531
IN CANADA: P.O. Box 603, Fort Erie, Ontario L2A 5X3

Want to try 2 free books from another series? Call 1-800-873-8635 or visit www.ReaderService.com.

---

*Terms and prices subject to change without notice. Prices do not include sales taxes, which will be charged (if applicable) based on your state or country of residence. Canadian residents will be charged applicable taxes. Offer not valid in Quebec. This offer is limited to one order per household. Books received may not be as shown. Not valid for current subscribers to Harlequin Presents books. All orders subject to approval. Credit or debit balances in a customer's account(s) may be offset by any other outstanding balance owed by or to the customer. Please allow 4 to 6 weeks for delivery. Offer available while quantities last.

Your Privacy—The Reader Service is committed to protecting your privacy. Our Privacy Policy is available online at www.ReaderService.com or upon request from the Reader Service. We make a portion of our mailing list available to reputable third parties that offer products we believe may interest you. If you prefer that we not exchange your name with third parties, or if you wish to clarify or modify your communication preferences, please visit us at www.ReaderService.com/consumerschoice or write to us at Reader Service Preference Service, P.O. Box 9062, Buffalo, NY 14240-9062. Include your complete name and address.

HP19R

"But…" Aislin couldn't form anything more than that one syllable. Dante's offer had thrown her completely.

His smile was rueful. "My offer is simple, *dolcezza*. You come to the wedding with me and I give you a million euros."

He pronounced it *"seemple,"* a quirk she would have found endearing if her brain hadn't frozen into a stunned snowball.

"You want to pay me to come to a wedding with you?"

"Sì." He unfolded his arms and spread his hands. "The money will be yours. You can give as much or as little of it to your sister."

It took a huge amount of effort to keep her voice steady. "But you must have a heap of women you could take and not have to pay them for it."

"None of them are suitable."

"What does that mean?"

"I need to make an impression on someone and having you on my arm will assist in that."

"A million dollars for one afternoon?"

"I never said it would be for an afternoon. The celebrations will take place over the coming weekend."

She tugged at her ponytail. "Weekend?"

"Aislin, the groom is one of Sicily's richest men. It is a necessity that his wedding be the biggest and flashiest it can be."

She almost laughed at the deadpan way he explained it.

She didn't need to ask who the richest man in Sicily was.

"If I'm going to accept your offer, what else do I need to know?"

"Nothing… Apart from that I will be introducing you as my fiancée."

"What?" Aislin winced at the squeakiness of her tone.

"I require you to play the role of my fiancée." His grin was wide with just a touch of ruefulness. The deadened, shocked look that had rung from his eyes only a few minutes before had gone. Now they sparkled with life, and it was almost hypnotizing.

She blinked the effect away.

"Why do you need a fiancée?"

"Because the father of the bride thinks going into business with me will damage his reputation."

"How?"

"I will go through the reasons once I have your agreement on the matter. I appreciate it is a lot to take in so I'm going to leave you to sleep on it. You can give me your answer in the morning. If you're in agreement then I shall take you home with me and give you more details. We will have a few days to get to know each other and work on putting on a convincing act."

"And if I say no?"

He shrugged. "If you say no, then no million euros."

Don't miss
The Sicilian's Bought Cinderella,
available February 2019 wherever
Harlequin Presents® books and ebooks are sold.

www.Harlequin.com

HPEXP0119R

HARLEQUIN
Presents®

**Coming next month—escape with this
spellbinding royal duo!**

**Read *The Prince's Scandalous Wedding Vow,* Jane Porter's
deeply emotional royal romance. Innocent Josephine finds
it impossible to ignore her instant connection to mysterious
Alexander—but will his royal secret change everything?**

When Josephine rescues a drowning stranger,
she's captivated. Until it's revealed he's Prince Alexander,
heir to the throne of Aargau… Now the threat of scandal
means this shy Cinderella must become a royal bride!

**Discover *Innocent Queen by Royal Command,*
part of Kelly Hunter's sinful and sexy Claimed by a King
miniseries. His royal duty must come before anything,
but will King Augustus be able to resist temptation?**

King Augustus is shocked when his country
delivers him a courtesan. But Sera's surprising innocence
and undisguised yearning for him pushes Augustus's
self-control to the limits. Now he won't rest until
Sera becomes his queen!

Available February 2019

HPBPA0119R